"You can stop calling me *Mr. Chatsfield*. That became redundant right about the first time I brought you to orgasm last night."

Orla gasped at his crudeness even as a hot flush seemed to sweep her from head to toe. "You're doing us no favors, *Chatsfield*. You're interested in taking my family's hotel business over purely because it suits some purpose of yours. And I'm going to find out what that purpose is."

Antonio's eyes flashed at her continued use of *Chatsfield* and he bit out acerbically, "Perhaps if you'd spent less time indulging that wickedly wanton siren you're so desperately trying to hide underneath that virginal suit today, you might be a little closer to figuring it out."

*Step into the opulent glory of the world's most elite hotel, where the clients are the impossibly rich and exceptionally famous.*

*Whether you're in America, Australia, Europe or Dubai, our doors will always be open....*

*Welcome to*

### The Chatsfield

*Synonymous with style, sensation...and scandal!*

For years, the children of Gene Chatsfield—global hotel entrepreneur—have shocked the world's media with their exploits. But no longer! When Gene appoints a new CEO, Christos Giatrakos, to bring his children into line, little does he know what he is starting.

Christos's first command scatters the Chatsfields to the farthest reaches of their international holdings—from Las Vegas to Monte Carlo, Sydney to San Francisco.... But will they rise to the challenge set by a man who hides dark secrets in his past?

Let the games begin!

Your room has been reserved, so check in to enjoy all the passion and scandal we have to offer.

Enter your reservation number:

00106875

at

www.TheChatsfield.com

### The Chatsfield

*Sheikh's Scandal,* Lucy Monroe

*Playboy's Lesson,* Melanie Milburne

*Socialite's Gamble,* Michelle Conder

*Billionaire's Secret,* Chantelle Shaw

*Tycoon's Temptation,* Trish Morey

*Rival's Challenge,* Abby Green

*Rebel's Bargain,* Annie West

*Heiress's Defiance,* Lynn Raye Harris

**Eight volumes to collect—you won't want to miss out!**

# *Abby Green*

—

## Rival's Challenge

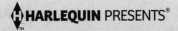

HARLEQUIN PRESENTS®

Recycling programs
for this product may
not exist in your area.

ISBN-13: 978-0-373-13279-9

RIVAL'S CHALLENGE

First North American Publication 2014

Copyright © 2014 by Harlequin Books S.A.

Special thanks and acknowledgment are given to
Abby Green for her contribution to The Chatsfield series.

HARLEQUIN®
www.Harlequin.com

**Printed in U.S.A.**

## All about the author...
### *Abby Green*

**ABBY GREEN** deferred doing a social anthropology degree to work freelance as an assistant director in the film and TV industry—which is a social study in itself! Since then it's been early starts, long hours, mucky fields, ugly car parks and wet weather gear—especially working in Ireland. She has no bona fide qualifications but could probably help negotiate a peace agreement between two warring countries after years of dealing with recalcitrant actors. Since discovering a guide to writing romance one day, she decided to capitalize on her longtime love for Harlequin® romances and attempt to follow in the footsteps of such authors as Kate Walker and Penny Jordan. She's enjoying the excuse to be paid to sit inside, away from the elements. She lives in Dublin and hopes that you will enjoy her stories. You can email her at abbygreen3@yahoo.co.uk.

### Other titles by Abby Green available in ebook:

WHEN DA SILVA BREAKS THE RULES *(Blood Brothers)*
WHEN CHRISTAKOS MEETS HIS MATCH *(Blood Brothers)*
WHEN FALCONE'S WORLD STOPS TURNING
  *(Blood Brothers)*
FORGIVEN BUT NOT FORGOTTEN?

This is for Suzanne Clarke—editor extraordinaire. One of the best ones. Thank you for your wisdom and guidance!

This is also for Dermot Cosgrove, who gave me invaluable insight into the French Foreign Legion— thank you! Any mistakes are purely my own.

# CHAPTER ONE

ANTONIO CHATSFIELD SENT silent *not interested* vibes to the lustrous dark-haired beauty sitting at the bar with her breasts displayed to prominent advantage in her low-cut dress, her kohl-enhanced eyes firmly on him.

Everything about her jangled at his sensitive nerve ends. She was too obvious. Too smooth. Too polished. This whole place was too polished. He cast a jaundiced glance around the dark and sensual bar space of his family's London flagship hotel. For the past decade he'd been used to surroundings that were more likely to be made of rubble and scented with the stench of chaos, death and panic. But he pushed those thoughts aside. *Not now.*

He'd chosen to come here for the dark corners and dim lighting as opposed to drinking himself into a stupor in the hotel suite which he currently called home. He smiled grimly to himself: at least he could appreciate the functionality of wanting to numb himself while in the presence of other humans. His therapist would undoubtedly approve.

That functionality had been hard fought for but even now the familiar feeling of skin-prickling clamminess was never too far away for him to forget completely—

the stomach-churning terror that used to grip him at random moments, sparked by something as minor as a dog barking or a loud noise, wrenching him out of the present and back to the cataclysmic past.

But the drink wasn't having much of an effect this evening. It was as if the acerbity inside him was diluting the effects. Even the woman lost interest now, turning her attention to another man who had just arrived at the other end of the bar. Antonio saw them exchange glances and saw the man indicate for the bartender to order her another drink.

Mentally he saluted them. He'd had enough encounters like that in his time. He just wasn't in the mood for one right now. Something spiked in his gut; he hadn't been in the mood for longer than he cared to admit, preferring to bury himself in work to avoid the gaping chasm inside him that he used to fill with meaningless encounters and high-octane danger.

He'd only been back in London for a couple of months, after years in exile, albeit punctuated by trips home. He was back because his family was in a state of crisis. His father had installed Christos Giatrakos as CEO to take charge of the family business—a worldwide string of eponymous luxury hotels that had been the byword in glamour and luxury since the 1920s.

The crisis was one of reputation and potential damage to the exclusive Chatsfield brand. Antonio's younger siblings, with the exception of his sister Lucilla, who had begged him to come and help, were all seemingly hell-bent on various forms of self-destruction amidst screaming headlines and lurid paparazzi shots. God knew, Antonio had indulged in his fair share of self-destruction along the way. He'd also left home when a lot of them were on the cusp of adulthood, so he could hardly judge them now.

Antonio had turned his back on his inheritance a long time ago and had had no intention of taking up the reins again, especially not when the autocratic Greek CEO wanted him to utilise his military and business expertise under the position of head of strategy to orchestrate the resurrection and expansion of the Chatsfield brand.

But his closest sibling, Lucilla, had begged him to reconsider, indicating that it would be the perfect position from which to help her topple the CEO. Apparently Giatrakos didn't know better than to let the enemy in through the front gate. And Lucilla's entreaties had called to that part of Antonio that still wanted to make things better. He felt that he'd left it too long to step in and offer to help his other brothers and sister, who were all fully fledged adults by now, but Lucilla had expressly asked him to help her. She wanted to prove to Giatrakos that they could restore the somewhat tarnished Chatsfield name by covertly taking over a rival hotel business, the Kennedy Group, before the shareholders' meeting in August, demonstrating that they had no need of an outsider. And if that meant coming back to a place he'd have preferred never to see again, then so be it.

A familiar ache grew in Antonio's chest to think of his siblings and how none of them, including himself, had ever really had a chance, let down by their parents long ago. He'd done his best for a while, but it hadn't been enough.

The old wounds of the blazing row he'd had with his father more than ten years ago were still vivid. That was when he'd realised how futile his efforts were and that perhaps the best thing he could do for his family was to walk away and let them get on with it. As his father had reminded him all too succinctly, Antonio wasn't his brothers' and sisters' father and never would be, so he might as well give up trying.

A mirthless smile touched Antonio's mouth. His sister Lucilla knew him well. She sensed the guilt he felt for having left his family when he had, even though she'd been the one to urge him to go. She also sensed his restlessness, his rootlessness. But perhaps most of all she was counting on his well-ingrained sense of responsibility still being partly intact. They'd been united in a heavy burden the day their mother had left their home, never to be seen from that day to this.

Antonio, despite all of the other mental images he'd accrued over the past decade, each one more horrific than the last, would never be able to erase the image of teenaged Lucilla holding their newborn baby sister in her arms, tears running down her cheeks. *Antonio, she's gone...just left us here. Alone.*

Antonio had been too angry and overwhelmed and *scared* to say anything, so he'd just pulled Lucilla and their baby sister into his arms, vowing to himself that he wouldn't let the family fall apart. Whatever it took. He was fifteen at the time.

Disgusted to find his thoughts deviating down that unwelcome path, Antonio downed his drink, telling himself he'd be better off in his suite after all and not infecting the clientele with his surly presence. After all, he *was* trying to help his sister....

But just when he was about to make a move from the stool, the door opened and a woman walked in and

Antonio's head blanked of any intention except to stay where he was.

He wasn't sure what it was about her that arrested him so powerfully. Maybe it was that she immediately stood out with her paler than pale colouring, made even more noticeable against the stark black of her dress. Maybe it was her long, slim, shapely bare legs and the classic black high heels. Whatever it was, Antonio couldn't move, his eyes tracking her graceful movements with a precision that had come from years of practice tracking targets that were far more lethal.

She came to the middle of the bar and waited patiently for the bartender to attend her. She had vibrant bright red hair, caught up in a high bun, showing off her delicate neck. A heavy blunt fringe was swept a little to one side; her eyes looked blue, but dark. Her dress was all at once discreet and sexy. It was silk and draped her from neck to mid-thigh, cinched in at the waist.

She had slender arms and delicate wrists. Short functional nails painted with clear polish. A black clutch bag. Diamond stud earrings and no other jewellery. Antonio realised that she wasn't as tall as he'd imagined—he'd guess about five foot four without the heels. Petite.

Instantly that awareness of her inherent feminine fragility caused a slow burn in his groin, sending blood to his penis, thickening and hardening the shaft of flesh. Antonio had to move slightly to accommodate his body, mildly frustrated that he was being so easily stimulated when he'd felt dead inside at the other woman's far more obvious charms.

From what he could tell under the loose-fitting silk of the dress, this woman's breasts were small. Maybe small enough not to wear a bra. Just then she moved slightly and Antonio realised that there was a slash in the front panel of her dress from the neck to just under her breasts, so discreet you mightn't notice, but he did. He also noticed a tantalising curve of one pale breast, pert and firm.

Desire engulfed him, swift and debilitating, as he imagined sliding a hand into that gap of material and cupping her breast, feeling the scrape of her hard nipple against his palm.

Orla Kennedy stood at the bar and tried not to let the prickle of self-consciousness make her run back out the original Lalique-panelled door of the seriously intimidating dark and decadent 1920s bar. She reminded herself stoutly that she was here for Dutch courage and to gain precious inside knowledge ahead of her meeting, so she couldn't give up just because she felt as if every single pair of eyes was on her, singling her out as a sad woman drinking alone. Or worse, she realised when she saw a man and woman obviously flirting at the other end of the bar, that she was here to pick up a man!

Orla glanced furtively around her, picking out some more couples at the intimate tables and a group of city boys in suits sitting at a table along the wall near the back of the bar. She breathed a sigh of relief that no one seemed to be laughing and pointing at her and decided to sit on a stool at the bar, noting that she could take in what was happening through the antique mirror on the opposite wall.

The handsome bartender put her drink in front of her with a wink and Orla thanked him, signing it to her room. She took a sip but still felt that slightly uncomfortable prickling sensation, as if someone was watching her.

Maybe it hadn't been a good idea to book a room at the Chatsfield Hotel ahead of her meeting with them tomorrow. She'd thought, in a light-bulb moment of inspiration, that it would serve her to get a measure of the people who seemed to be intent on taking over her own family's ailing hotel business. Not that she needed to stay at the hotel to know of its well-documented luxuriousness and exclusivity.

However, its reputation had taken a dent in recent times, thanks to the scandalous exploits of the Chatsfield heirs and heiresses. Orla's soft mouth firmed to think of how they seemed determined to acquire chains in distress. Namely, the Kennedy Group, started up and owned by her father. He'd begun in Ireland in the sixties with a small hotel in the west of Ireland and through sheer grit and determination had built up an empire— helped along by the famed boom years. By then Patrick Kennedy had moved operations to England with his wife and young daughter, Orla.

Unfortunately the economic downturn hadn't been kind to them and a series of hotel closures had severely diminished their overall worth, making them vulnerable to takeover bids. They were nowhere near the league of the Chatsfield empire, but Orla could see how they would be an attractive prospect to add to the Chatsfield portfolio, as they weren't too far removed with their good reputation and discreetly exclusive clientele. Which was why she was here now, trying to get a feel for their adversary. And, she realised with a sinking feeling, all it was doing was driving home just how intimidating a task she was facing.

The feeling of being watched was so intense at that moment that Orla looked to her left and the breath left her mouth in a gasp when she saw a man deep in the shadows, at the corner of the bar, watching her intently. He didn't look away. And, to her rising mortification, neither could she.

It was the shock of colliding with that dark unsettling gaze, of not noticing him before now, that held her enthralled. She wondered how she could have missed him. He commanded the space around him. He was dark and broad. Short thick hair. Dramatic masculine features. Almost harsh. An unsmiling grim mouth, but full lips, his top one slightly fuller, and suddenly Orla was fixated on his mouth, and wondering what it would feel like to have those unsmiling lips touch hers.

The realism of what she was doing—staring at a complete stranger's mouth and wondering what it would be like to kiss him—hit Orla squarely in the chest and she almost fell off the stool she was so embarrassed. Cheeks flaming, she swung her guilty gaze back to her drink and then knew she couldn't stay there spotlit under the bar's lights, dim as they were.

Aghast that the man might have misconstrued her look, she gathered up her bag and the drink and moved to one of the tables against the wall which was covered in dark opulent velvet. She chose to sit at the wall, on the banquette seat, and breathed a sigh of relief to be slightly more hidden, cursing herself that she hadn't had the sense to just come in and choose a seat and let her order be taken.

She noticed her heart was thumping harder than usual, a queer fluttering low in her abdomen, and looked over to where the man was again, confident that he wouldn't see her now. But she could see him and he was still looking at her. Orla's pulse raced. She'd never experienced this before. It felt earthy, wicked, *sexy*.

Against the silk of her dress, her bare breasts peaked, making tremors of awareness shoot up and down her body. She'd only realised when she'd unpacked that she hadn't brought the bra she had to wear with this dress. And she'd *had* to wear the dress as she didn't want to look too conspicuous in the bar in the trouser suit she'd brought for the meeting tomorrow.

She'd figured that the loose material would hide the fact that she was braless as she was lucky enough, or *un*lucky enough, that her breasts were on the small side. But now, she felt as if she might as well be naked and was acutely aware of the gap in the material which usually showed only a discreet glimpse of the bra but which would now show skin if someone looked hard enough. *Like the man.* He'd been looking hard enough. Instant heat moistened between Orla's legs and she squirmed.

She resolutely diverted her gaze from the man and looked down, hunching her shoulders slightly for fear of giving anyone else the slightest bit of encouragement.

On top of all of the awareness coursing through her body which she couldn't seem to dampen down was the disbelief that she had even attracted the gaze of such a man. From what she'd seen he looked like the type who would go for the far more busty lady who was now practically sitting in her partner's lap. Any minute now they would leave and Orla felt a twinge of something like envy for a second before squashing it with disgust.

OK, so it had been a while since she'd had sex. More than a year to be precise. And it had been a good while before that, if ever, that she'd had any kind of sex to write home about. And maybe she had never had a relationship that lasted longer than a few weeks. But the men she met didn't seem so enamoured when they found out that her passion for her family business came first.

Orla had contented herself that her career was her bedfellow. And up till right now it had been perfectly satisfactory. If a little lonely and frustrating when she saw amorous couples come into her hotel for romantic weekends and then leave a couple of days later looking sated and dreamy-eyed. So why was she thinking of this all of a sudden and feeling hot and unsatisfied inside?

Because of a stranger's blatantly interested gaze. *God.* What was wrong with her? He was probably the type of guy to hook up with anything with a—

'Do you mind if I join you?'

Orla's head snapped up so fast she heard a bone crack in her neck. For a second it was as if someone had just hit her. Everything receded and then rushed back. The man was standing there. In a dark suit and white open-necked shirt. He was astonishingly gorgeous up close, and he was enormous. All over. Ridiculously tall…six foot three? Six foot four?

Orla was so stunned that she couldn't speak. He clearly took that as encouragement and sat down opposite her, in the velvet upholstered bar chair. She could only gape at him. His sheer nerve. The fact that he was right there in front of her.

He put his drink on the small table and that seemed to jolt Orla back to some kind of reality. She looked to the left and right and then hissed in his direction, 'I did *not* say you could sit down.'

Her heart was beating so fast she was breathless. Giddy with a rush of something that felt disturbingly like excitement. Disgusted at herself for this rampant reaction, she went to stand up but the man just said urgently in a deep and mesmerising voice, 'Please don't leave.'

His voice tugged at her nerve endings, making them tingle. Orla stopped and looked at him. She felt breathless all over again. He really was huge. Broad and powerful. Even more arrestingly masculine up close, his features defined and stamped with virility. And then she realised his accent wasn't foreign. She frowned. 'You're from here?'

He nodded. 'Yes. Why?'

'You just…' Orla went hot in the dim light when she realised she was giving away the fact that she'd thought about him for more than a fleeting moment. 'You look foreign.'

His mouth tipped up on one side, drawing Orla's eyes to it.

'I'm half Italian, half English.'

'Oh…'

'And you?'

Almost slightly stupefied, Orla answered, 'Irish… born there but brought up here.'

'That would explain your red hair.'

Orla looked into his eyes and wondered what colour they were. They appeared black in this light and she shivered slightly, suddenly aware of a hardness to this man she'd not noticed before. A latent sense of danger.

And then she remembered where she was and stiffened again. 'Would you please leave? I did not ask you to join me.'

There was a taut silence between them and he didn't

move. Huffing, Orla made to move again. 'Fine, well, if you can't have the courtesy to move, then I will.'

But his hand snaked out and wrapped around her wrist and Orla felt as if a lightning bolt of heat went straight to her groin.

'Please…you'll be doing me a huge favour if you can just pretend that we know each other for a minute.'

Orla looked at him. Speechless and not just because of his hand on her wrist that felt hot and *big*. She pulled free and held her arm to her chest in an unconsciously defensive gesture. She narrowed her eyes on him. 'What are you talking about?'

'See that woman at the bar?'

Orla glanced over to where he had inclined his head slightly and saw the woman who *had* been wrapped around the other man like a vine. He was gone and she was alone again.

'Yes, I see her,' Orla supplied somewhat reluctantly.

'Well, I'm afraid that I was going to be next on her hit list.'

Orla looked at the man and her eyes widened. He had a look on his face that was downright…pathetic. Big eyes, all innocence. Orla felt a very scary falling sensation inside her chest. *He was flirting with her.* Outrageously. Her nipples tightened into hard tight buds and Orla crossed her arms for fear they'd stand out like beacons against the thin silk of her dress. She put on her most severe expression. The one that usually had staff scurrying in all directions.

'And you're trying to make me believe that you're not strong enough to stand up to a little bitty woman?'

He lifted a brow and that elevated his face from gorgeous to downright sexy. 'Not working, no?'

Orla shook her head and couldn't stop her own mouth twitching ever so slightly. She saw movement behind the man and observed dryly, 'I think you're safe now—her current victim looks like he was just on a toilet break.'

The man didn't look behind him, but Orla realised when he looked up that he could see through the reflection of the venetian glass over the banquette seat as it was tilted slightly down towards the seating area. He looked back at her and smiled. 'There goes my cunning ruse to have an excuse to talk to you.'

Butterflies exploded in Orla's belly. She could insist on getting up to go, but right now she was curiously loath to. This man was a smooth charmer, but he also had an intriguing rough edge too, and there was no doubt about it, but something deeply feminine within her felt like it was blossoming in the heat of his regard. Coming back to life.

As if sensing her weakening, he said, 'Can I buy you a drink for disturbing your peace?'

Orla hesitated. She had the funny sense that her peace was about to be disturbed in a very profound way. And that if she pushed for him to leave again he'd go. There was something innately proud about him.

But what harm was a drink? Feeling sensitised and more alive than she could remember feeling in a long time—*if ever*—she uncrossed her arms and shrugged minutely and took a mental step over a line. 'Sure, why not?'

As if like magic, to prevent her changing her mind, an immaculately clad waiter appeared to take their orders. The man didn't take his eyes off Orla and the waiter left. She was feeling breathless again, all hot and liquid inside.

A very feminine dampness was growing between her legs and she crossed them in a moment of self-consciousness. His eye immediately went to one pale thigh and Orla cursed her choice of dress. She put her hands on her leg and he looked back up, a smile making his mouth quirk again as if he knew exactly how awkward she felt.

He sat back. 'So…tell me, you're here on business?'

Orla nodded. She really didn't want to get into anything that reminded her of the reality she faced. The inevitable takeover of her family business. So she said, 'I'm in sales…'

Which was pretty much true. Along with marketing, management, PR, entertainment, travel, diplomacy…

The man grimaced and said, 'I'm in acquisitions. It's a grind, isn't it?'

Orla regarded him suspiciously. This man looked no more like a banal businessman caught up in the daily grind than Santa Claus in full flight with all the reindeer. But she sensed intoxicatingly as if they'd both tacitly agreed to pretend to be something, someone, else.

She was about to respond when something unpalatable occurred to her. She glanced at his left hand and didn't see a ring, but that didn't mean anything. 'Are you married?'

He shook his head and the faintly sick expression that passed over his features assured her even more than when he said, 'No…'

Then he frowned. 'Are you?'

Orla shook her head quickly and repressed a shudder. No way was she ever getting married so that some

man could come and take half of the business she'd
worked so hard to build up with her father. She'd seen
the detrimental effects a marriage had on a business.
'No,' she said quickly, emphatically.

'Well, as we've established that we're both free and
single...where were we?'

Orla repressed a shiver of awareness, of pure physical longing, and the feeling that she wasn't in control
of what was happening at all. She forced her mind to
operate. 'We were in sales and acquisitions, I believe.'
*And why did that suddenly sound so...suggestive?*

'Ah, yes...'

The waiter returned then with their drinks. Whisky
for both of them.

The man lifted his glass and tipped it towards her.
'To chance encounters.'

Orla lifted her glass too, and said, 'To very forward
men with pathetic chat-up lines.'

He smiled. And so did she. They took a drink and
Orla relished the smooth feel of the liquid running down
her throat. Warming her up. She felt unbearably sensual
all of a sudden. Languorous.

'Perhaps we should exchange names?'

Orla's chest tightened. Names were real. They would
root this in reality and she suddenly didn't want that.

Far more lightly than she felt, she said, 'I think in-
troductions are overrated. We'll most likely never meet
again. What's the point?'

His eyes glinted in the dim light. A tiny smile tipped
up one corner of his mouth. 'We don't have to divulge
real names if you don't want to. But I would like to call
you...something.'

Orla went hot again. So that he could call her something in the throes of passion? The wicked thought made her pulse spasm between her legs.

He held out a hand then, a mischievous look in his eye. 'I'm Marco.'

Orla put her hand in his and for a second her mind blanked when his big one enclosed hers completely. When she felt the calluses on his skin.

'I'm…Kate.'

'Nice to meet you, Kate…?'

Orla smiled at his obvious query as to her second name and pulled her hand free. 'Just Kate.'

He nodded. 'Kate Kate, it is. And I'm Marco Marco.'

*Lord.* No man Orla had ever met came close to this man. He enveloped her in sexual awareness. She felt energised. Alive.

'You have a meeting here tomorrow?'

Immediately Orla rejected another reminder of reality. She shook her head. 'Let's…not talk about tomorrow.'

He went still and his eyes narrowed on her face. She could see him look at her mouth and she imagined she could feel it tingle.

He said with a rough edge to his voice, 'No real names and no tomorrow. You're right. The present is so much more interesting.'

He leant forward, glass in his hand. 'I was about to leave when you walked in.'

Orla's heart hitched. 'You were?'

He nodded. 'But then I saw you and I stopped.'

Mesmerised by his dark gaze, Orla asked faintly, 'Why did you stop?'

'Because you captivated me.'

'Oh…' For a long moment she said nothing, could

only look at his mouth as a tight wire of need seemed to link to the insistent throbbing between her legs.

'This is where you say you noticed me too...' Marco supplied helpfully.

Orla's eyes rose. She felt dizzy. She was losing it. No longer herself. 'I didn't see you at first.... I don't know why.'

The man's mouth flattened for a second. 'I was hidden. In the shadows.'

Orla nodded slowly. Something touched her—as if what he was saying had a deeper resonance. 'You were.... That's why I didn't see you. At first.'

Orla couldn't stop talking. 'And then when I did...I couldn't look away.'

She blushed now and clasped her drink in two hands. 'But I didn't want you to think I was encouraging you.'

'Don't worry,' came the dry response. 'You gave a fairly frosty signal to stay away.'

She looked up, incensed. 'I'm not frosty!'

He got all heavy-lidded. 'I know...'

Orla went hot all over. Her nipples ached now they were so tight. Her belly clenched with need. She'd never been this turned on in her life.

The bar space was like a dark decadent cocoon. Orla glanced around and noticed that the table of men had left. So had the amorous couple at the bar. There was only one other remaining older couple, and she hadn't even noticed. She felt a jolt of shock.

Marco lifted his glass and downed what was left of his drink in one go. For a second Orla had the wrenching sensation that he was going to leave and the feeling of rejection of that idea stunned her. She didn't even know this man!

He put his glass down and Orla took a quick fortifying sip of hers. He looked at her for a long intense moment and she couldn't even break the tension because it resonated within her. She wanted this man with an urgency that was completely alien. And thrilling.

His voice was deep. 'I wanted you from the moment you walked in. I want you so much I ache with it. And I can't remember the last time I wanted a woman this badly.'

Orla's mouth went dry. The sum total of their physical contact so far had been his hand on her wrist to restrain her from leaving, but she knew that if he put his mouth anywhere near hers she would go up in flames.

Something about his brutal honesty connected with her. It was so much more seductive than if he'd insisted on some meaningless patter for another half an hour when they both knew that what was happening between them was crazy. Unreal. Unprecedented.

Feeling shaky at the thought of even contemplating what she was contemplating, Orla said, 'I...I want you too.'

His eyes flashed and the throbbing heat between her legs intensified and she had to fight to stay still when she wanted to move around and ease the ache somehow.

She blurted out, 'But...I didn't come down here to meet someone, for a one-night stand.'

He looked deadly serious. 'I know.'

His eyes on hers, hypnotising her, he said, 'I'm going to get up and pay for these drinks at the bar. If you want to leave, I won't stop you. But if you don't...'

He didn't have to finish. If she didn't...she would spend the night with this man. In his bed. After a long charged moment, he stood up, reminding Orla of just how powerful and tall he was, calling to that deeply feminine part of her that exulted in the sheer biology of a potentially strong and virile mate. She'd never met someone so intensely masculine who made her feel so *female*.

Then he turned and went to the bar with a fluid grace that made Orla stare after him helplessly. Her mind went into turmoil. She had so much to think about—papers for the meeting tomorrow that she should go over. The reality of facing the demise of her family business. And yet, right here, right now, it all seemed very far away and not that important.

Somehow she got up and grabbed her bag. She was struggling to hang on to sanity, elusive as it was. She felt hot, feverish. Excited, scared. She couldn't just let this man take her to his room. It was crazy, ridiculous. Dangerous.

Determined not to be led by her suddenly out of control hormones, Orla intended to leave the bar so that when he finished paying she'd be gone.

But just when she drew level with the tables nearest the bar she couldn't help looking up and her gaze clashed immediately with a dark one reflected in the mirror behind the bar. Her heart stopped. Her breath got short and choppy.

His face was unreadable, those eyes so dark that she couldn't make out the expression, but she couldn't look away. Much like when she'd seen him first.

She realised that he'd already paid. He'd been watching her for the past couple of minutes, waiting to see what she'd do. Giving her the chance to go if she wanted to. And suddenly, something deep inside her rebelled. Broke free. She wanted this man so badly she ached all over. So she stood there. Didn't move. It passed between them, unspoken but there. *Yes.*

Slowly he turned around and the full force of his physicality hit her between the eyes. Without a word he came towards her and took her free hand in his. Then he led her out of the bar.

In a daze, Orla let him lead her to the lift. Once inside they were alone. To her surprise, he let her go and leant back against the opposite wall. In the brighter lights of the lift he was even more intimidating. His skin was a dark olive, his eyes a very dark brown. For a second sanity threatened to return and then as the lift ascended he said in a low rough voice, 'Show me your breast.'

His voice was commanding and any remaining sanity melted away and was replaced with heat. For a second Orla couldn't take in his words and then she followed his gaze and looked down to see where her dress was gaping open slightly, showing skin.

Infused with a heady and hot sense of something very wicked, Orla lifted her hand and slowly pulled one side of the silk dress open, revealing one pale breast. Her fingers brushed against her tingling nipple and she had to bite her lip to stop a sound of reaction coming out of her mouth.

She stared at him, her cheeks burning with a mixture of shame and intoxication. His eyes were black, smouldering, cheekbones darkening with a rush of blood. Her nipple tightened, the aureole puckered.

The lift shuddered lightly to a halt. Marco's eyes glittered as he dragged his gaze back up. Orla dropped her hand and the dress went back into place. The doors opened and he took her hand again, tightly, leading her out. She almost had to jog to keep up with his much longer stride.

He stopped at the end of the corridor and opened the door with a key card. They went in. Orla dimly registered that the room was palatial and had an astounding view. As soon as the door closed behind them, Marco let Orla's hand go to rip off his jacket, throwing it in the direction of a chair.

Her back was against the door. He turned to face her and she looked up at him, in awe all over again at his sheer size. He made her feel tiny, delicate. Desire pounded through her in waves.

He stopped for a second and asked tautly, 'Are you sure you want this?'

Orla had made her decision back in the bar when she'd met that black gaze in the mirror. She swallowed and tried to inject her voice with as much insouciance as she could muster considering this was the boldest thing she'd ever done in her life.

'I'm here, aren't I?'

# CHAPTER TWO

*I'M HERE, AREN'T I?* The sparky husky words washed over and through Antonio, ratcheting up the exquisite knife-edge of arousal in his body. He'd never been brought so close to the edge before, when he'd barely touched this woman!

For a split second something inside him contracted when he realised just how far out of his zone of control he already was, but he couldn't focus on it. All he could see was this woman's, *Kate's*, mouth, plump and kissable.

He put his hands on the door over her head, caging her in slightly, angling his body forward. She was looking up at him, eyes huge. Lashes long and dark.

'Take down your hair.' He wanted to see it fall around her shoulders.

After a slight hesitation she lifted her hand and huffed slightly. 'Has anyone told you you're awfully bossy?'

Antonio's mouth quirked when he thought of the platoons of elite soldiers he'd commanded. 'Frequently.'

She pulled at something and then her hair was falling down in soft silken skeins around her shoulders, its colour vivid even in the dim light. Antonio dropped a hand and took some strands between his fingers. He'd never felt anything so fine, so soft. A dim and distant damaged reflex of his memory wanted to break this moment apart but he wouldn't let it rise. He utilised the exercises that had brought him back from the brink of madness and focused on her, on her smell. Musk and roses. All at once ethereal and earthy.

Unable to resist the torture any longer, he let her hair slide through his hand and trailed his fingers across the delicate line of her jaw. He saw the pulse quicken at the base of her neck and felt his body throb in response.

Tipping her chin up with only the slightest of pressure from his fingers, he dropped his head and his mouth touched hers. Sensations exploded behind his eyes. Hers were still open too, dark blue. He'd noticed that in the lift. Like dark violets. Emitting a growl at his own restraint which was barely hanging on by a thread, he closed his eyes and deepened the kiss, feeling that lush mouth soften even more under his, opening to him, inviting a deeper intimacy.

When their tongues touched it was like an electric shock. He felt small hands reach out to grab his shirt; his chest shuddered at even that fleeting touch. Unable to hold back from what he'd wanted to do all evening, Antonio dropped his other hand and found the gap in the front of Kate's dress. He slid his hand in and cupped her bare breast, feeling the hard nub scrape his palm, and he felt feral with need, cupping, squeezing that flesh, fingers pinching at the peak, making it harder. Her skin was like silk. Warm and soft.

Through the roaring of blood in his head, he could feel her body moving closer to his, hear her moans coming from deep within her. He caught her round the waist with his arm; she felt tiny and fragile and it called to

something deeply masculine within him, a primal part
that had gone long unused. The material of her dress
was slippery and he pulled her into him, against where
his flesh was so stiff and hard.

Orla dragged her mouth from Marco's and gazed into
glittering eyes. She was breathing hard. She was plas-
tered against him, on tiptoe, and she could feel him,
long and hard and thick, against her belly. Her mind
blanked. She knew he was a big man. But he felt *huge*.
An explosion of damp heat made her even wetter.

He was breathing harshly too, his chest moving rapidly. His hand was still on her breast.

Feeling completely wanton, Orla got out roughly, 'I
want to see you.' She could give orders too.

Marco drew his hand out from under her dress and
Orla had to bite her lip not to grab his hand and put it
back on her hot flesh. Slowly he started to undo his buttons and Orla's eyes followed their progress as his chest
was slowly revealed bit by bit. Her eyes widened when
he pulled his shirt off completely and it fell to the floor.

*Magnificent* was too banal a word for the perfec-
tion in front of her. He was a warrior. Surely descended
from ancient warriors. His chest was massive. Rock-
hard. Muscles clearly delineated and rippling. Dark hair
dusted his pectorals and descended in a line under the
belt of his trousers. Orla's gaze dropped farther and she
saw the bulge pushing against the material. She gulped.

'Now you,' came the throaty command.

Orla looked up again. Mouth dry, she reached behind her for the small button at the top of the back of
her dress. She released it and held the dress in place for

a moment before taking a deep breath and letting it fall forward and down, held in place now only by the belt.

Marco's gaze felt hot on her skin. Her breast that he'd touched still throbbed.

'You're so beautiful.' He reached out a hand and traced the aureole of her other breast with a finger. Orla bit back a groan, her eyes closing because it was sensory overload to take in both the sight of him and the feel of him. Her skin puckered tight.

And then her eyes flew open and she gasped with shock when she felt the hot sucking heat of his mouth. Orla's hand went to his head, fingers stabbing deep into thick hair. His skull was hard and his mouth was pure wicked torture. She sagged back against the door, her legs increasingly shaky.

'Marco…' she panted. 'I don't think I can keep standing.'

Her legs were wobbling in earnest now. He lifted his mouth off her breast and she cursed her weakness. But then he straightened and scooped her into his arms as if she weighed no more than a feather. She put her hand to his chest, the muscles bunching and moving under her palm. For a woman who prided herself on being strong and authoritative, being held like this struck at that deep feminine chord within her.

He carried her in through the suite to the bedroom where one small lamp was on by the bed. Orla noticed stuff around the place—books, clothes—but she barely took it in; the strength and power in the body that held her was awesome. She faintly wondered if he might be an athlete.

Marco put her down on the bed and trailed his hands down her legs, slipping her shoes off so they fell on the floor with a soft thud. Then those hands came back up her legs and he pushed them apart, standing between them, at the edge of the bed.

Orla's breath quickened. His hands were on her thighs now, huge. His thumbs climbing higher and higher to where her body would tell him just how badly she wanted him too.

She felt embarrassed by what her body was about to reveal. Impetuously she said, 'Don't!'

He stopped. 'Don't what?'

Orla turned her head away, desire thick in her body, but feeling exposed in a way she'd never felt before. No man had ever made her feel this out of control.

In a small voice she said, 'I don't want you to know....'

'Know what?'

She looked back at him, the words trembling on her lips—*how much I want you*—but she held them back, saying instead, huskily, 'I don't even know you.'

Marco's hands didn't move. He just stared at her in the dim light and then presciently answered her unspoken words. 'I know.... It's the same for me.'

He took his hands off her thighs and immediately Orla wanted them back on her. Instead they were on his belt and he was opening it, sliding it through the buckle with a sibilant hiss of leather through fabric. Now he was opening his trousers, hands disappearing under the waist, pushing them down, taking his briefs with them.

All the breath in Orla's body seemed to disappear as she took him in. Massive and aroused. Moisture beading at the tip of his erection.

'See...' he said with a funny tight quality to his voice, 'how much I want you? It's mutual.'

He came between her legs again and Orla could only lie back and let him replace his hands on her thighs. They moved upwards until they formed a V at the juncture of her thighs. She fought not to squirm against them, as if to guide him to touch her more intimately.

And then, his eyes smouldering, he pulled aside her panties and stroked his fingers along her very damp cleft. He said something in a language she didn't understand. It sounded guttural, French. But not like any French she'd ever heard.

She closed her eyes, her entire body going as taut as a bowstring as he stroked her and then slipped a finger inside her. Her back arched off the bed; she gasped out loud, hands clenching at thin air.

He came down beside her, the bed dipping with the weight of his big frame. One finger became two inside her and his mouth found her breast and suckled roughly. Orla wanted to scream. She was spiralling faster and faster towards the peak, her hips jerking against his hand. And without warning it broke over her and inside her, the most powerful orgasm she'd ever experienced. It was so mind-altering that she wondered if what she'd experienced before had even been an orgasm.

Marco's hand stilled against her as her pulsating body came back to earth. Orla felt disorientated; she opened her eyes and saw him like a Greek god beside her. His hands went to the belt on her dress and he undid it, far more dextrously than Orla would have managed it right now. To her mortification, she knew she was trembling with the force of what had just happened.

Then he was pulling back and tugging her dress down over her hips and off. Now she wore only her panties and he slipped them off too. Orla saw him reach

for something and heard a ripping sound. A condom.
He was about to smooth it onto his erection and Orla
felt a burst of desire. 'Wait.'

He stopped and looked at her and she could see what
pleasuring her had cost him when she could see the
sweat on his brow, the strain on his face.

A wicked inner sorceress she'd not known she even
had inside her said, 'Let me.'

Tonight she was *Kate*. Tonight reality didn't exist, or
it did but it was part of a fantasy she wasn't even aware
existed in her mind. Tonight she could be someone else.

She came up on her knees, thankful that they didn't
collapse because all her limbs felt like jelly. She took
the condom out of his fingers and came closer to the
edge of the bed. He was so tall that all she had to do
was reach out and roll it over that thick length, the veins
standing out in bold relief under delicate skin.

Orla bit her lip when she hit the base of his shaft,
and then his hands were on her arms and he was gently
pushing her back down onto the bed, her legs folding
underneath her.

'Sweetheart, if you keep touching me and looking at
me like that, this will be over before we've even started.
I can't hold on.'

Marco scooted her back onto the bed, and pushed her
legs apart and lowered his body into the cradle of hers.
Holding her breath, Orla felt that thick head push into
her body, stretching her, impossibly. Even though she
couldn't have been more ready. She sucked in a breath
and felt him thrust a little deeper.

'You're so small. I don't want to hurt you.'

He was. Almost. But not quite. Orla was hovering on

the threshold between pain and pleasure. She drew up her legs beside his thighs and said, 'You're not.'

Something about his concern and the gentleness of someone so huge made Orla feel quivery inside. She wouldn't have expected it of him from that first intimidating sight of him in the shadows of the bar.

He thrust a little deeper and the pain flared for a second before being replaced with something more tantalising. Slowly, Marco started to move in and out, his chest rubbing against Orla's breasts, making their sensitised tips tingle.

Her breath got quick again. She moved her legs to wrap them around his hips and he slid deeper. He still wasn't in all the way though, and he moved his hand between them, his thumb finding that sensitive clump of cells and rubbing rhythmically against her, making her moan.

And then he slanted his mouth over hers, and as if a dam broke within her, Orla felt something release, and Marco slid deep inside her, touching every single nerve point in her body. Or at least that was what it felt like.

Her legs tightened reflexively around Marco's lean waist, her body spasmed with a rush of pleasure and as he thrust in and out their tongues sucked and licked and tasted. They were joined at every possible point and Orla truly didn't know where she ended and he began because it felt for the first time in her life as if she was whole, as if a missing part of her had slid home.

The tempo increased and Orla could feel her body clasping at him with the onset of another orgasm, even more powerful than the last. Their bodies grew slick with perspiration. Orla dug her heels into Marco's hard muscled backside and with a strangled roar he thrust one final time, the tendons in his neck standing out as they both hovered on the brink of something earth-shattering. And when it hit them simultaneously, it was like a force of nature, sweeping everything aside, obliterating any previous experience in the blinding white heat of pleasure.

Antonio blacked out for a moment. Literally lost consciousness. And then came back to himself within seconds, breathing harshly, his body embedded in Kate's... held in her tight clasp. He could still feel the spasmodic pulsations of her inner body around his length and extricated himself with a wince of pain and pleasure.

He looked at the woman under him; she was staring up at him with the same stunned expression that he figured was on his face.

He rasped out, 'OK?'

Silently, she nodded. Her cheeks were flushed, hair a tangle of glorious red around her head. Antonio found it within himself to move so that he could pull the covers over her. And then he said, 'I'll be back in a second.'

He stood up, and to his consternation, his legs felt distinctly weak as he walked to the bathroom where he dealt with the protection. He stood at the sink afterwards and looked at himself. His face was flushed too, eyes glittering brightly. But he felt altered in some indefinable way. Which was crazy. It had been sex. Just sex. The hottest sex he'd ever had, a small voice pointed out. Even so, it was just sex.

He'd hooked up with women like that many times before, preferring short encounters with mature, experienced, willing females with no strings attached. This was no different. They hadn't even told each other their real names, for crying out loud! But it felt different. He rubbed absently at his chest where he felt an ache growing and frowned at himself. Splashing water on his face, he cursed this moment of introspection and went back into the room to see Kate on her side, curled up, facing away from the bathroom. And the ache in his chest intensified. *Had he hurt her?* She was so small.

He padded over and pulled back the cover, sliding into the bed. He saw her shoulders tense and something in him rejected that. He needed to see her. He put a hand on her shoulder, feeling the delicate bones, and tugged gently. After some resistance, she rolled over, holding the sheet over her chest.

She was pale now, biting her lip. Eyes huge. Antonio felt a punch to his gut. 'Did I hurt you?'

She shook her head and said in a low voice, 'No. It's just…I've never… It's never been like that. For me. So intense.'

Relief made the feeling in Antonio's gut subside. He couldn't help a small smile as he automatically reached out to push some hair back from her smooth cheek. 'Me too.'

She narrowed her eyes then and said with a touch of acerbity, 'I bet you say that to all the girls.'

Antonio looked at her. 'And I bet you say that to all the guys.'

She shrugged a shoulder minutely. 'Maybe.'

A lightness infused the atmosphere now, dispelling the intensity of a few moments ago, and Antonio growled softly, 'You'll pay for that.'

And then the implication of what she'd just said hit him and suddenly the thought of another man touching her made him see red. It made him gather her into his body and clamp his mouth to hers with a feral sound from deep within him. He didn't want her to think of *any* other man after tonight. Only him. He wanted to brand himself on her.

With a soft sigh he felt her resistance melt away as their kisses got more and more heated, the fire in their bodies igniting again. The sheet was quickly dispensed with and Antonio drew Kate's slim supple body over his, spreading her thighs either side of him.

Urgently before he donned protection he asked, 'Are you too sore?'

Kate had her hands braced on his chest, her arms pushing her small pert breasts together and forward. Everything in Antonio was screaming for release. Already. *Again.* It made him nervous because he couldn't remember ever feeling like this before, but he couldn't think about that now.

She shook her head, tendrils of hair slipping over her shoulders like flames of fire. She moved back, teased him with her body. Antonio put on the protection, his hands uncustomarily clumsy, and then slowly, torturously, exquisitely, brought Kate down onto his aching shaft.

He saw stars as her tight damp sheath took him in. He saw the fierce concentration on her face, their eyes locked. And then she started to move against him and Antonio could do nothing but submit and surrender to the wild ride once again.

When Orla woke up, tendrils of the dawn light illuminated the room in a faint pink glow. Birds tweeted, and through the open curtains she realised there was a terrace outside the bedroom. A very opulent and luxurious bedroom. Not her bedroom. *His* bedroom. A Chatsfield bedroom with its signature bespoke furnishings.

It all came rushing back. Along with the realisation that her body ached all over and she was tender between her legs. *Very* tender. She blushed to think of taking him into her body, how big he'd been. How good it had felt.

Orla held her breath and turned her head. Marco lay beside her; they weren't touching. His huge body was in a louche sprawl, completely naked. Wide awake now, Orla came up gingerly on one arm, wincing as muscles protested.

They'd made love over and over again. And each time had felt like she was falling deeper and deeper into a vortex of need. Even now, as her gaze drifted over his face, she felt that need rising. In spite of the tenderness between her legs. She'd take that burn again.

A shadow of stubble darkened his hard jaw. He appeared no less intimidating in repose. Just as fierce. Orla's eyes widened though as she looked down his body and saw a veritable patchwork of scars and marks. There was a bunch of very distinctive circular puckerings of flesh around his pectorals. She mustn't have noticed them before because it had been dark—she blushed—and she'd been too intent on succumbing to the most intense desire she'd ever felt.

There was a tattoo high on the biceps of the arm nearest her. It looked like a coat of arms. He had the body of an elite athlete…or a warrior. Her impression of last night came back, even more forcibly in the light of dawn, gazing at his scarred body. Literally from neck to knee, there were all kinds of marks—healed cuts, stitch marks. Those mysterious circular shapes.

There was a particularly ugly gash around one muscular thigh that looked as if it had healed badly.

For the first time Orla had a very real sense of just how irresponsible she'd been. Maybe he was some kind of criminal? The thought sent shock waves through her body as she recalled how he'd been hidden in the shadows of the bar. How he'd come over and stopped her from leaving. How easily he'd enraptured her. She'd barely put up a modicum of resistance!

She gazed around the room. Something cold went through her as she took in details. It looked lived in. Books. An old edition of *Aesop's Fables* stood out oddly amongst them. Clothes. Paraphernalia. More than an overnight visitor like herself. She'd noticed it last night but hadn't really taken it in.

The assertion took root. He was living here.

*Who was this man?* A sense of urgency gripped her now. She had to get away. She'd almost forgotten entirely why she was even in the Chatsfield Hotel. How could she have forgotten? She'd never allowed herself to get so sidetracked from work before.

Ashamed and angry with herself for being so impetuous, so *selfish*, Orla slid off the bed as quietly as she could. To her intense relief, Marco didn't move. She was terrified that he'd wake. That he'd open those dark compelling eyes and she'd be lost again. Orla picked up her dress and pulled it on with trembling hands.

She found her bag. No matter how hard she searched though, she couldn't find her panties. Marco moved minutely on the bed and Orla's gaze froze on that huge rangy body. With sick fascination she couldn't help looking at the most potently masculine part of him. Even in sleep he was awe-inspiring. He moved again and panic took her breath. She had to leave *now* before he woke. Wrenching her gaze away from the sleeping man, she turned and went to the bedroom door.

Unable to help herself though, she stopped at the door and looked back. A fierce tug of something that felt awfully like regret made an emotion she didn't like to name rise up within her. Before it could surface she clamped down on it and turned away again and left the suite. It was only as she was walking down the corridor that she realised she'd left her shoes and the belt of her dress behind, along with her missing panties.

Exactly four hours later Orla was tapping her pen impatiently on the thick blotting paper pad that sat in front of her on the table. Her legs were crossed under the thick varnished oak table in the conference room and her leg jigged back and forth nervously. Even though the room was modestly sized, there any comparison to a normal hotel conference room ended. It exuded plush luxury. Everything one might require for a meeting was there, but discreetly tucked away so nothing jarred. Orla's nose wrinkled. She'd noticed a scent in the air when she'd checked in yesterday but then had forgotten about it when she'd been so effectively distracted.

But now she noticed it again and suspected waspishly that the Chatsfield Hotels must pump their signature scent throughout their premises, thereby increasing the whole *Chatsfield* experience. It was a smart strategy. Smell was well known to be one of the more powerfully evocative senses, and so by having a scent that linked people's memories indelibly to you was prime subliminal advertising. She'd looked into it for their own hotels but it would have been too expensive.

The Kennedy Group solicitor checked at his watch again and his counterpart across the table said smoothly, 'I'm assured that Mr Chatsfield is on his way, and as I've said, he regrets keeping you waiting.'

Orla huffed. She just bet he did. No doubt this was part of the strategy to let them know how weak they were and who was the power player here. It didn't help, of course, that she felt woefully underprepared considering her very out of character sexual adventures last night with a complete stranger who could very well be some kind of underground criminal or a mercenary.

When she thought of all those scars and markings on his body though, she didn't feel scared so much as...*hot*.

She imagined her wanton behaviour must be tattooed on her face like a beacon for all to see but she hoped that the effort she'd put into hiding the ravages of the night before had worked. She'd asked her assistant to buy her some shoes on her way over that morning, claiming some feeble excuse that the ones she'd brought wouldn't go with the dark navy trouser suit she wore.

So now she had brand-new shoes biting into her feet on top of everything else. She put down the pen and fiddled nervously with her white shirt and hoped that the frill detail down the centre where the buttons were didn't appear too frivolous. She'd been more frivolous in the past twelve hours than in her entire life. And she was not frivolous. Her mother was frivolous. Flighty. Selfish. Orla was hard-working, serious. Frugal.

She'd pulled her hair back into a sleek ponytail and her heavy fringe offered the faint illusion that she could hide behind it.

Just then they heard voices out in the corridor and all the tiny hairs all over Orla's body seemed to stand up on end for no apparent reason. The door opened slightly and a huge dark shape loomed just out of sight.

Then the door opened fully and a man walked in with another man in tow. A cold seeping horror spread through Orla's body. Shock knocked the breath out of her chest. She couldn't believe her eyes. He was striding in now, clad in a pristine three-piece dark suit that hugged his huge muscular frame. His jaw was clean-shaven. He was stupendously gorgeous. Arresting. Sexual charisma was a tangible aura around him.

Orla was dimly aware that her own assistant had straightened in the chair beside her. The unconscious action of a woman in the presence of a virile alpha male. In spite of being in her middle-aged years with a healthy brood of children and a loving husband.

Orla felt a surge of something that made her want to turn to her assistant, one of her best friends, and snarl at her.

And then the man's eyes fell on the people waiting for him. And one in particular. *Her.* He stopped in his tracks on the other side of the table. That dark compelling gaze on hers. She saw the shock in their depths before it was quickly veiled.

Her lungs burned because she hadn't drawn a breath. A million things seemed to lodge in her throat and in her belly: mortification, embarrassment, anger. Shock. *Desire.*

The Chatsfield solicitor was standing now and saying, 'Antonio, I'd like you to meet Orla Kennedy of the Kennedy Group, her solicitor Tom Barry and her assistant, Susan White. Miss Kennedy, I'd like you to meet Antonio Chatsfield and his assistant, David Markusson.'

Orla was dimly aware of the people either side of

them both standing to reach across the table to shake
one another's hands. She was paralysed. Her mystery
lover was Antonio *Marco* Chatsfield. The eldest son
of the notorious Chatsfield family. She had read up on
him prior to this meeting. Ironically he was almost the
only one of whom there were no recent photos as he'd
been in the army and then the secretive world of private security for years.

If he'd joined the regular army Orla might have
seen pictures. But he hadn't. He'd joined the famed
and mythic French Foreign Legion and had served with
them for seven years. It was where one entered and as-
sumed another identity. Highly secretive and closed to
the outside world. Effectively Antonio Chatsfield had
been a ghost until his recent return to the family fold.

But he was no ghost. He was very solid and very
real and he was looking at her now and waiting for her
to do something. Orla's brain felt sluggish with shock.

Her assistant, Susan, discreetly nudged her with her
foot, under the table. That physical contact seemed to
jolt Orla out of her fog and she stood up and put out her
hand, her training and innate manners dictating the au-
tomatic moves of social training.

After shaking hands with his assistant, her hand was
clasped in his much bigger one—tightly—and the fire
of his touch seemed to explode the memory box open
in Orla's brain and body. She was barely able to hold
back the onslaught of a thousand lurid images: writh-
ing underneath him, sobbing, panting, gasping. Clenching her legs tighter around his hips, begging him to go
deeper, *harder*.

'Miss Kennedy,' he said in that deep voice. His eyes
had darkened to black and Orla imagined she could see

veritable sparks shooting her way. Something in her hardened as she pushed down those images to a deep place of personal shame. She gripped his hand back just as tightly.

'Mr Chatsfield.'

He didn't let her go. He drawled, 'It's funny but I could have sworn we've met somewhere before.'

Hot mortification threatened to swamp Orla but she refused to let it rise. If her eyes could have killed, he'd have been vaporised on the spot. She gritted out, 'Believe me, Mr Chatsfield, *we've* never met. I think I would have recalled it, as your family are so memorable.'

Antonio Chatsfield's eyes flashed at that none too subtle barb and his hand was so tight on hers now that Orla could feel her bones grind together. She bit back the need to cry out. And then abruptly he released her. Orla wanted to cradle her hand to her chest but didn't, not wanting to show him a moment of vulnerability.

There were two of them who'd conspired to pretend to be someone else last night. He had no right to lambaste her silently for it, or allude to it in front of these people.

He said with a deceptive lightness which surely had to be meant only for her ears, 'I must have been mistaken, then, because the woman I'm thinking of is called Kate.'

Orla's face paled even more when she saw the curious look of her assistant from out of the corner of her eye as she sat back down. Her second name was Kate. They'd both used their second names. It wasn't even funny.

# CHAPTER THREE

THE MEETING PASSED in a blur, with much of the discussion revolving around complicated legalese talk between the solicitors. In those instances Antonio sat back in his chair and regarded Orla steadily, forcing her to try and glare him out, refusing to be intimidated. She had nothing to be ashamed of, she assured herself stoutly. She always ended up looking away first though, as those eyes brought her back in time to only a few hours before and she couldn't halt the lurid images from taking over.

He positively radiated hostility and at one stage Susan leant close and said *sotto voce*, 'What's up Chatsfield's nose? I'd heard he was charming…but he's looking at us as if we're something he found on the bottom of his shoe.'

Not *us*, Orla replied silently, *just me*. And the more he sent out those silent vibes, the angrier she got.

The Chatsfield solicitor was looking at everyone around the table now. 'Well, it would appear as if everything is in order for us to begin negotiations regarding a potential takeover of the Kennedy Group.'

Orla saw the smallest of smirks play around Antonio Chatsfield's mouth and something inside her blew up. She stood up and put her hands on the table and stared straight at him. 'With all due respect, I disagree. From what I've seen here today I'm not sure that I want to continue discussions of a possible takeover by the Chatsfields.'

Orla heard her assistant and solicitor gasp simultaneously. She felt quivery with rage inside. He was playing with her, punishing her. She hated this feeling of vulnerability and exposure.

Antonio stood up too, and after a long taut moment he said to the others without taking his eyes off Orla, 'If you would excuse us please, I'd like to speak in private with Miss Kennedy.'

Orla cursed herself and her big mouth. And her red-haired Irish temper which her father had always told her originated from her fearsome grandmother who had had ten children and almost outlived them all.

The solicitors and assistants left the room hurriedly as if sensing the powder keg of tension about to go off between Antonio and Orla.

The door shut behind them and they were alone. Tendrils of shock still coursed through Orla to be face to face with the mystery lover she'd never expected to see again.

Antonio stared across the table at his lover from last night and wanted to smash the table aside and throttle her. Or kiss her. Despite the anger he'd felt as soon as he'd realised who she was, his body refused to react along the dictates of his head. It was as rampantly in lust with her as it had been since the moment he'd laid eyes on her.

She looked nothing like the wild and wanton woman who had urged him with that low husky voice to take her *harder*, *deeper*, over and over again just hours ago.

Her body coming apart under his with an intensity that had driven him so far over the edge he'd blacked out.

No, Orla/*Kate*, appeared as cool as a cucumber in a fitted short-jacketed trouser suit and white shirt with a very feminine frill detail. Buttoned to the neck like some Victorian heroine. Vibrant hair pulled back and sleek. That heavy fringe highlighting the exquisite prettiness of her face. Her dark blue eyes.

What had made him even more incandescent during the meeting was the very uncomfortable knowledge that he'd slept like a baby while she'd sneaked out of his room. Antonio never slept through anything. It would have meant life or death in his line of work. Yet, she'd managed to get out of his bed and get dressed and leave the room. As if he'd been drugged.

He'd almost missed the meeting because he'd slept so long and had only woken when Lucilla had rung him, wondering why he hadn't shown up for their pre-meeting meeting.

Antonio forced himself to utilise years of training to keep his emotions at bay. He crossed his arms and saw her throat move as she swallowed. She crossed her arms too, and he hated the involuntary reflex of his eyes when they dropped momentarily to the pushed-up swells of her breasts under her shirt.

Cursing himself, he looked at her. 'I suppose you found it amusing?'

She frowned. 'Found what amusing?'

Antonio's lip curled at her wide-eyed innocence. 'To seduce the man who intends to take over your crumbling empire?'

She gasped and her cheeks went pink, which had an immediate effect on Antonio's body, forcing him to grit his jaw against the rise of desire, blood already pooling in his groin, making him hard.

Her eyes flashed a brilliant affronted sapphire blue. 'I did *not* know who you were—you flatter yourself, Mr Chatsfield. If I'd known who you were last night I would have walked right out of that bar and kept walking. I do not need to sleep with opponents the night before a meeting to get my kicks.'

Antonio felt a hard mass settle in his gut. 'So it's just the thrill of sleeping with random strangers, then?'

Her cheeks went even pinker. 'How dare you judge me when you were the one who seduced *me*.'

Antonio snorted inelegantly. 'Give me a break. You came down to that bar looking for something and it wasn't to sit alone and have a drink. You might not have been as obvious as that other woman but you were just as effective.'

Orla recalled brazenly showing him her breast in the lift and clamped down on the torrid memory. Her chin came up. 'And I suppose you were there for nothing else but the good of your health? You were quick enough to come and proposition me when I gave you no encouragement whatsoever.'

Antonio ignored that and raked her with a scathing glance. 'I see you've eschewed your peek-a-boo little black number for the meeting. You cannot seriously expect me to believe that you weren't up for it when you came into that bar in a dress designed for seduction in mind. You weren't even wearing underwear.'

Orla's arms dropped and Antonio saw her clench her hands to fists and recalled gripping her hand tightly as anger had engulfed him, and the excoriating feeling of exposure. No woman had ever walked away from him before. He moved around the table, not even really sure of what he intended to do. He just wanted to provoke Orla.

Her eyes got wider. The blood in his body leapt. She put out a hand. 'Don't come near me, I mean it. How dare you accuse me of being *up for it* just because of how I was dressed. That's very close to the kind of thing men say to justify their actions when accused of—'

'Don't even say it,' Antonio ground out, incensed that she would even frame such a thing. And yet, she had a point. His brain was so entangled from seeing her here like this that he was being reduced to acting from some visceral place, saying things that he would never normally utter. He didn't like to be reminded of how he'd gone over to her last night. The thought that she hadn't wanted him as badly as he'd wanted her was like acid in his gut.

'Damn you, Orla.'

It was the first time he'd said her name and it made Orla feel funny inside. His scent enveloped her, woodsy and mysterious. Exotic. She could feel the vibrations of anger leaping between them.

She reacted. 'Damn *me*? That's hardly fair, is it? We're both to blame for what happened.'

She didn't want him to know how he'd filled her head since she'd walked away from him that morning. How regret had built in her gut, making her feel like she'd made a huge mistake.

After a taut moment of silence, he walked over to a nearby window which overlooked a London park. He put his hands in the pockets of his trousers, inadvertently drawing the material of his pants taut across his muscular buttocks. When he turned around abruptly, guilty heat rose up Orla's chest and she glanced away hurriedly.

Antonio sighed heavily and said, 'You really didn't know who I was?'

Orla looked at him, still affronted. 'Of course not. How unprofessional do you think I am? And I did not go looking for a one-night stand either. *And* that dress happens to be perfectly respectable—it's from a well-known designer.'

She went even hotter as she admitted with extreme reluctance, 'I do have something to wear underneath it, but I forgot to bring it with me. And I didn't want to look too conspicuous in this suit.'

Antonio leant back against the window frame now and crossed his arms over his chest again. 'So you were scoping out the competition.'

Orla pursed her lips and said nothing but then Antonio raised a brow and she realised that if she didn't admit the truth then how could she justify going to the bar to drink alone? Even though there was nothing inherently wrong with that.

Angrily now she admitted, 'Fine, yes, I wanted to get a feel for your hotel and business.'

She glared at him mutinously. 'But I got sidetracked. Perhaps you knew who *I* was, Mr Chatsfield, and you were seeking to distract *me*?'

He shook his head, his face unreadable. 'I didn't know who you were. In fact, I was under the impression that your father was coming to this meeting, not his daughter.'

Fire racing up her spine, Orla said, 'And no doubt you would have preferred to meet with him than a mere woman?'

Antonio's eyes flashed. 'I'm not a misogynist, Orla,

so don't pin that label on me. I don't have a problem dealing with you over your father as long as you're up to the task…and right now let's just say that the information I have to go on is rather more weighted in the personally intimate department than business.'

Cheeks burning at that, Orla met Antonio's gaze with as much froideur as she could muster when she felt as if she was on fire all over. 'Well, I hate to have to remind you that the feeling is mutual. I've never had a one-night stand in my life, and believe me, as experiences go it's right up there in the "never to be repeated" column.'

Orla took up her briefcase and turned to go but was caught by the arm.

She looked back to see Antonio's face hard with displeasure. 'Don't think I didn't get that impression when I woke up to find the mysterious *Kate* gone. But not for a second do I believe that last night wasn't as pleasurable for you as it was for me. Our bodies didn't lie, sweetheart, and if I kissed you right now I could have you flat on your back on that table in seconds.'

Orla's blood got hot at the vivid image that invaded her mind of being splayed across the table. She wrenched her arm free. 'Of all the egotistical arrogant jerks… This meeting is most definitely over, Mr Chatsfield. Last night was a huge mistake. I wouldn't let you take over our business now if you offered triple what you're offering to buy us out. And I wouldn't sleep with you again if you begged me.'

Those last words were needless and childish but Orla felt sick inside to acknowledge just how far off her own rigid tracks she'd gone after last night. She'd wilfully jeopardised everything for a fleeting moment of pleasure.

Antonio stood back and Orla was once again struck

by his sheer size compared to hers. She hated feeling so fragile. *But you didn't hate it last night*, a small voice mocked. No. She'd revelled in it.

His gaze was disdainful as it swept her quickly up and down. 'I've never begged for sex in my life and I don't intend to start now. And I wouldn't be so quick to cut off your nose to spite your face—you need us. I don't see any other hotel chains rushing to your aid. Who else has the resources we have in these straitened times to dig you out of the hole you're in?'

He wasn't finished. 'And I think you can give up *Mr Chatsfield*—that became redundant right about the first time I brought you to orgasm last night.'

Orla gasped at his crudeness even as a hot flush seemed to sweep her from head to toe. She was losing it. 'You're doing us no favours, *Chatsfield*. You're interested in taking us over purely because it suits some purpose of yours. And I'm going to find out what that purpose is.'

Antonio's eyes flashed at her continued use of *Chatsfield* and bit out acerbically, 'Perhaps if you'd spent less time indulging that wickedly wanton siren you're so desperately trying to hide underneath that virginal suit today, then you might be a little closer to figuring it out.'

Orla's hand lifted and it had cracked across Antonio's cheek before she'd even realised her intention. He didn't even flinch. White with fury and shock at her unprecedented physical violence, Orla swung around and stalked out of the room, her entire being suffused with humiliation and anger.

Antonio looked at the door, the slam resounding in his ears. Damn the woman. He should never have allowed a part of his anatomy to dictate his actions last night, no matter how intense the attraction. His cheek burned after her slap but he welcomed it. He deserved it for being so reckless. So downright unthinking. And he knew he deserved it for what he'd just said. He'd lashed out because he was angry with himself. She was right; he'd pursued *her*. And he knew that she could have been wearing a sack last night, and today, and he'd still want her.

He swung around to the window again and cursed volubly. Because of this moment of supreme weakness on his part, he could fail his sister. This was the only thing she'd asked of him: to initiate a takeover of the Kennedy Group and prove to their newly installed autocratic CEO that they had it within them to expand, in spite of negative publicity and their badly dented reputation.

When he'd left to join the Legion, Cara, their baby sister, had been only ten. Little more than a child. Antonio couldn't go back in time and rewrite history or suddenly reappear in his siblings' lives as if nothing had changed. He may have kept an eye on them over the years, but that wasn't the same as being there, being present.

But he was here now and his priority was to support his sister and, in so doing, his family also, no matter what. And if that included taking over Patrick Kennedy's hotel business, which was ripe for the picking, then so be it. He could do this. This was easy compared to what he'd been through.

So he would not let some slip of a woman get in his way. No matter who she was or how much she turned him on. That was a purely physical and chemical anomaly. He could control it. He had to. Because as surely as night would follow day, Orla Kennedy would be back with her tail between her legs. Because she had no choice.

And when she came back, Antonio would be waiting.

'Are you sure this is our only option?' Orla tried to hide the panic she was feeling. She looked at their solicitor and he sighed volubly.

'No matter how many times you ask the question, Orla, the answer stays the same. Yes. A takeover by the Chatsfields is our only option to avoid out-and-out bankruptcy right now.'

*'Right now.'* Orla seized on this glimmer of hope. 'If we can hang on for a little longer—'

Tom cut her off. 'You'll have nothing to hang on to. Time is of the essence. If we don't look at their offer seriously they could well take it off the table completely. And no one else has their resources.'

Orla paced back and forth in her office. It had been a week since her cataclysmic night and that disastrous meeting with Antonio Chatsfield. And all week she'd been trying to work out some way to avoid ever having to see him again. Which, she knew, was entirely selfish and resulting out of her own reckless behaviour which made it even worse.

Tom asked now, 'You know the longer you drag this out, the more likely your father will hear of it? He thinks that negotiations are under way.'

Orla wrung her hands together and stopped pacing to face their solicitor. He looked stern. Her belly sank like a stone.

Tom went on. 'Once he's finished selling off your assets in South-East Asia he'll be back and expecting to hear good news. You know how important it is to him that the Chatsfields agree to an integrated takeover and the stipulation that the UK and Ireland Kennedy Group hotels keep their name? Not to mention the last remaining New York Kennedy hotel.'

Orla nodded miserably. Tom didn't have to spell it out. She was jeopardising everything she had worked so hard for. Her father was already sick with guilt at the bad business decisions he'd made—against Orla's repeated entreaties to do otherwise.

Orla had done her best ever since she could remember to be there for her father, ensuring that he had the support he didn't get from her mother. When she had been about nine years old she'd overheard her father talking with his business manager, late one night after a party. He'd said sadly, 'Marianne can't have any more children…so it's just Orla. If we had a son to leave it all to, then there might be a chance…but I just don't see how we can expect Orla to fulfil that role.'

Orla knew now that her father was innocently old-fashioned in his beliefs about women's roles but she'd vowed since that day to work extra hard to prove to him that she could take on the burden. And she'd excelled at it. Working at their hotels at every opportunity—after school, weekends, school holidays. Sitting in on her father's meetings, largely unnoticed but soaking everything in. Gaining a master's degree in hotel management by the incredibly young age of twenty-three.

In the end her sex had made no difference. Her hypervigilance and diligence hadn't been able to stop her father from being influenced by his need to keep his pleasure-and luxury-loving wife happy.

They'd been living beyond their means for so long now that this offer from the Chatsfields was their only option. The sick circling in Orla's brain came to a halt. *Their only option.* The knowledge sank like a stone in her heart.

She looked at Tom and sighed heavily. 'Very well. I'll go back…but I'll go and see him alone.'

Orla didn't want witnesses to the potential humiliation Antonio Chatsfield was about to serve up to her.

'Miss Orla Kennedy is here to see you.'

Antonio did not like the jump of his pulse to hear this annoucement or the anticipation that sizzled in his veins to think of her outside his office right now. Curtly he answered, 'Send her in.'

Good manners prompted Antonio to stand up when he would have preferred to stay sitting, as much to disguise any bodily reactions he was afraid he might not be able to control as an effort to demonstrate a position of power. Not that he even agreed with pathetic games like that. That was more his father's style.

He went and stood by the window and waited, forcing his blood to cool. The door opened. 'Miss Kennedy, sir.'

Steeling himself, he finally turned around, but despite his best efforts his body reacted as if it was made of iron filings and a magnet had just walked into the room. It was that physical a sensation.

'Thank you, Maggie,' he managed to get out, and vaguely heard his secretary say something about bringing refreshments. Orla Kennedy looked pale. There were shadows under her eyes. Her hair was up in a bun at the back of her head and it reminded him forcibly of that first night he'd seen her. She was dressed today in a dark green knee-length shift dress and matching jacket, black heels. The green made her Celtic colouring look even more dramatic.

To his intense irritation he could feel the blood pooling in his groin, stiffening his flesh as he imagined pulling her into him, removing her jacket, pulling down the zip at the back of her dress....

Moving before he could embarrass himself, Antonio went back around his desk and indicated the high-backed seat on the other side. 'Please, take a seat.'

Orla walked in, her face set and stern. Mouth compressed. Clearly as loath to be facing him again as he was to be facing her. She put down a briefcase and sat down primly on the chair.

Just then a knock came and Maggie reappeared with a tray holding tea and coffee. Antonio forced himself to smile at the woman and said, 'We'll take it from here, thank you. Please see to it that we're not disturbed.'

When she'd left, Antonio looked at Orla, who had two flags of pink in her cheeks now. His groin throbbed. 'Tea or coffee?' he gritted out.

'Tea, please.'

That husky voice. Just hearing it again brought back the X-rated dreams he'd had to endure every night for the past week. Reminded him of waking in damp sheets, his body painfully aroused and aching for fulfillment.

He poured the tea and handed her the cup and saucer which she took quickly, putting it down in front of her with a clatter of crockery. The pinkness in her cheeks intensified.

Antonio poured his own coffee and took a sip, willing his body to behave.

Orla ignored her tea. She looked so tense she might break in two. And then she blurted out, 'Look, Mr Chatsfield, I regret what happened between us that night, as I'm sure you do too. I think we're both agreed that if we'd known who each other was, it never would have happened. I just…I just want to put that night behind us and start again. Pretend it didn't happen.'

There was such an earnest expression on her face and her eyes were so huge that Antonio almost felt sorry for her. Almost. But something wicked and hot inside him chafed at her insistence on calling him by his surname, and that she regretted it, or that they could put it behind them. Even though he'd been telling himself all week that he regretted it.

Faced with her now, separated by only a desk, with his body throbbing with need, Antonio couldn't be anything less than completely honest.

He sat back and regarded her steadily. 'I would have to disagree. And do I need to remind you why you should stop calling me Mr Chatsfield?'

Orla blanched. She looked at the man sitting behind the desk, supremely relaxed and confident, and struggled to hold in the rise of her temper. Especially when she thought about the sleepless nights she'd endured all week, because every time she closed her eyes all she could hear was her heartbeat and imagine his huge body, pressing hers down into the bed, filling her, stretching her….

'I take it you received your belongings?'

Orla's temper went up a notch. 'Yes, thank you,' she said tightly, acknowledging receipt via courier of her missing belt and shoes, but *not* her panties. Face burning now, she refused to even ask the question.

But as if reading her mind, Antonio said, 'There was one other item but I felt it might be the kind of thing you'd prefer was discarded rather than returned.'

Orla went puce and wanted to hit him all over again. Choking back the humiliation she'd fully expected but not thought would come from this direction, she got out, 'A gentleman would not even bring that up.'

He smiled and it was so explicit it sent shock waves of sensation down to Orla's pelvis.

'Ah, but I never claimed to be a gentleman. I don't think you were very interested in me being a gentleman that night, any more than you were interested in being a lady.'

Orla glared at him, incensed and insulted. 'I came here, hoping to appeal to your professionalism, but it's clear that this is just an exercise in futility.'

'You came here,' he pointed out silkily, 'because you have no choice if you want to save your precious family brand name and a fraction of your fortune.'

Orla's insides cramped at that reminder. Feeling sick, she said bitterly, 'I am aware of that fact. I'm not here to discuss errors of judgement, so if we could just focus on the business at hand....'

Determined to maintain things on a business footing when it felt as if her grip on control was woefully shaky, Orla bent down to open her briefcase and removed a sheaf of papers.

She placed them on the table beside the tray of tea and coffee, avoiding Antonio's black gaze.

'Some of our terms have changed slightly. I've added in a requirement that you, or one of your staff, comes and sees how our business model works first-hand before anything is signed. Our name will live on and as such we want to be sure that our standards and reputation for excellence of service will be maintained.'

After a few seconds of silence Orla risked a look at Antonio. His face was hard, inscrutable.

'That could be easily avoided by the removal of your name and replacing it with the Chatsfield one.'

Orla struggled to maintain her composure. He was just trying to unsettle her; this was one of the first things her father had stipulated before even agreeing to think about the takeover bid.

She tried to keep the panic out of her voice. 'You know that's one of the fundamental staples of this agreement. That our hotels keep their name. Which is why we need to ensure that excellence is maintained.'

Antonio stood up and Orla had to crane her head back he was so tall. He walked around the table and her heart thudded when she thought he was going to perch on the edge of it. Far too close for comfort. But then he went and stood at the window, hands in his pockets.

His back looked impossibly broad, tapering down to those lean hips, hard buttocks and long, powerful legs. Orla had a memory flash of the scars dotted all over his body and felt weak inside. Obviously they'd come from his time in the army.... She didn't like the way she felt slightly sick to think of how they'd come about.

In a moment of weakness during the week, she'd delved further into her research of him and had discovered that he was a decorated war hero. It hadn't made the general news because it had been as the result of a covert mission with the Legion.

He turned abruptly and Orla's mouth dried.

'If your father was so concerned with excellence, then how the hell did he let the business run through his fingers? Along with us and a few others, the Kennedy Group was one of the few predicted to withstand the recession. Now you'll be lucky to keep the name.'

Orla felt sick. No way was she going to get into the sordid details of her father's weakness for indulging his wife and her extravagant ways.

She stood up, not liking how intimidated he made her feel. Loath to blame her father, Orla said, 'We made a series of bad decisions. And yes, we had a cushion to protect us for a while, but once the downturn hit, those decisions cost us...too much.'

Antonio was grim; he crossed his arms. 'It was more than that. You know we've had your accounts to inspect as part of this deal. It was a veritable haemorrhaging of money and ludicrous decisions. How on earth could your father have ever believed it would be a good idea to expand into South-East Asia with a brand that was aimed primarily at this domestic market and America—which had very clear advantageous links due to the solid Irish/American connection?'

Orla looked away. That decision was the one that had put them over the edge. She'd begged her father to reconsider his South-East Asian plans but her mother had insisted that it was where they should be. She'd fancied the kudos of hotels in Hong Kong and Bangkok. Orla had known it was suicide.

Bravely, she lifted her chin. 'My father...*we*,' she quickly amended, 'got the best advice at the time, projected earnings and we were assured that it was a good idea.'

Antonio shook his head. 'I've been out of this game for some time, I'll admit. But anyone with half a brain cell could have foreseen that disaster.'

Orla burned inside because she agreed with every word he said. Anyone would have known it, except a fool in love like her father. She'd long ago despaired of her mother's ability to skew his judgement and it had taught her to steer well clear of something similar happening to her. Never would she be so blinded by emotion in business. *So what happened the other night?* a small voice jeered in her head. That had been *lust*, Orla told herself fiercely. Not emotion.

Hating the way her throat suddenly felt tight, she said stiffly, 'I don't really see the benefit in discussing why we're in this position. I'm more interested in discussing the future.'

To her intense relief, Antonio shrugged one broad shoulder minutely and went back behind the desk to sit down. He pulled her sheaf of papers towards him and began to flick through them with long fingers.

Orla sat down again too, and her heartbeat returned to some semblance of normality. Well, what was normal for her around this man which was still *ab*normally fast.

He glanced up once he'd flicked through them all. He was almost bored. 'There's nothing new here.'

Orla swallowed. This was her chance to try and claw back some control. 'I know why it's so important to you to gain control of the Kennedy Group.'

Immediately Antonio looked dangerous, reminding her of what she'd sensed when she'd first met him.

'You do.' It wasn't a question.

She nodded. 'You want us because we're vulnerable

but also because you're trying to prove to your CEO that you don't need outside help to restore confidence in your brand.'

'And how—' Antonio's voice was lethally soft '—did you figure this out?'

# CHAPTER FOUR

ORLA FELT HOT in her jacket. She longed to take it off but didn't dare. 'The tabloids follow your family all over the world. It's been rumoured that your new CEO has been instructed to find roles for the family in various meaningful positions, in order to contain the negative public image.'

Antonio was positively glacial now. 'Do I strike you as the sort of person to bend to another's will?'

Orla quivered inwardly at the thought of him bending to *her* will…in the bedroom. She shook her head quickly as if that could dispel the incendiary thought. 'No,' she had to admit reluctantly. Her theory seemed to fit for everyone else, but he was right. Not Antonio. He was a self-made millionaire who ran one of the world's most secretive and successful security companies.

Orla lifted her chin. 'Nevertheless, family loyalty, or something, has put you in this position. The truth is… Antonio…' Orla hated how saying his name felt so intimate. 'The truth is that we need each other.'

The ice in Antonio's eyes disappeared and was replaced by heat. Instantly Orla cursed her choice of words.

'I couldn't agree more,' he drawled.

Furious at herself for allowing that lazy opening,

she said, 'I don't mean like that. What I mean is that you need me to agree to this takeover just as much as the survival of our name needs *you*, the Chatsfields.'

Orla crossed her arms and refused to let him intimidate her with those hot and cold looks. 'And I'm not saying yes to anything until you agree to come and see how we work and sign an addendum to the contract that puts my father on the board as a member so that he can ensure the protection of our reputation.'

Now Antonio was furious. 'There's been no mention of your father being allowed to sit on the board.'

Orla stood up, relishing doing something that might dent this man's insufferable arrogance even for a moment. 'Well, there is now.'

Antonio stood up too, and advanced around the table, making Orla's brief feeling of triumph dissolve in a pathetic rush of heat to her core.

He stopped just inches away from her and she found it hard to breathe or think clearly. What had he just said? All she could see was that formidable body and the stark gorgeous lines of his face. His mouth. All she could feel was her body going on fire.

'Seeing as how we seem to be negotiating all sorts of new items, perhaps you can tell me how we're going to negotiate this?'

*This* was Antonio coming closer and reaching for Orla with one big hand around her waist and the other at the back of her head, and before she had time to say a word or do anything, he'd pulled her against his hard body and his mouth was on hers in a bruising passionate kiss. She was welded so tightly against him that she could feel the hard thrust of his arousal against her belly and just like that her brain went molten.

The pent-up sexual frustration of the past week meant Orla had no defence for this sensual attack. She went up in flames. Her arms were around Antonio's neck, hands clasping his head, fingers tunnelling through silky thick hair, before she could even stop herself.

It was as if someone had lit a match to a bone-dry piece of tumbleweed. Antonio boldly thrust his tongue into Orla's mouth and she sucked it deeper, relishing the way his body jerked against hers. Here, at least, they were equal.

Orla's breasts felt swollen and sensitive, nipples stinging and chafing against the lace of her bra. Antonio was dislodging her hands and arms, pushing her jacket off her shoulders and down her arms. She felt a slight breeze glide over hot skin but even that wasn't enough to douse this insanity.

There was something desperate in their mutual combustion.

Their mouths were welded together, Orla's hands exploring the powerful width of Antonio's shoulders, and down, over his rock-hard biceps, lingering, squeezing.

When her dress suddenly felt looser around her chest Orla barely noticed; it was only when she felt a tug that she realised that he'd pulled the dress down her arm and half off. He finally broke away from the kiss.

Orla felt dizzy. She opened her eyes reluctantly to see Antonio's flushed face, his burning gaze on her lace-covered breast.

His arousal was hard against her; he brought up a big hand and cupped that lace-covered mound of flesh and squeezed gently. She almost whimpered. When his fingers pulled down the delicate material and her breast popped free, and he pinched her tight nipple, she couldn't keep the feral sound in.

He swallowed that whimper of need with another kiss, grinding his hips into her, making her want to spread her legs. But she couldn't in the confines of her dress. As if sensing her frustration, Antonio reached for and pulled up the bottom of her dress, over her thighs. Manoeuvring her with powerful ease, he sat her back on the edge of the desk and came between her legs, his erection now moving rhythmically against her swollen and moist mons covered only by the thinnest of cotton barriers.

Antonio broke away and muttered thickly, 'I need to be inside you.'

Orla's heart clamoured. She was ready to plead, beg, for him to do exactly that as fast as he could and then something interrupted their heavy breathing. A phone ringing. Her mobile.

They both stilled, the piercing ring cutting through the fog of heat and lust, finally defusing it and bringing back sanity. Even so, Orla had to acknowledge how close she'd been to begging this man—whom she'd only met today for the *third* time in her life—to take her on the side of his desk, in his office. If she'd ever had a chance of regaining some tiny sliver of dignity after last week, it had just melted.

Orla pushed at Antonio's rock-hard abs and scrabbled to pull her bra and dress back up, hands shaking. With a guttural curse Antonio took a step back. Orla realised her hair was down around her shoulders. She felt acutely sensitised all over, skin tingling, a dull throbbing ache between her legs.

'Orla,' he began, and she looked up, glaring at him, trying to do her zip up with clumsy hands.

'Don't,' she got out fiercely, 'say one word.'

'Let me help you at least,' he said tightly.

Cursing out loud because she knew she couldn't reach her zip by herself, Orla turned around. Antonio lifted her hair out of the way, and that made a violent shiver run through her body. The backs of his knuckles skimmed her spine as he drew the zip all the way up.

As soon as he was done she bent down and retrieved her jacket and put it on. She would just have to leave her hair down. Antonio walked around to the other side of his desk. When Orla had her jacket on and was holding her bag she looked at him. His face was stark, unsmiling, and something suspiciously tender inside her tugged. She clamped down on it. She had no desire to see this man smile—where had *that* come from?

'Don't look at me like that.' He growled softly, making Orla's skin tighten all over again.

'Like what?' Her voice felt rusty.

'Like what just happened wasn't mutual.'

Orla glanced down at the sheaf of papers. So much for keeping things businesslike. She looked back up. 'I need to get back.'

Antonio did smile now but it didn't reach his eyes. Again that funny tug near her heart.

'Running away, Orla?'

Orla grabbed her bag in front of her with both hands. 'Not at all. I've said what I came to say. I'll leave you to think about it, but we both know you don't have much choice…if you want my agreement for this takeover to happen.'

Antonio leant forward and put his hands on the table. Now he seemed positively devilish. 'There's one aspect of this takeover I'd be most happy to explore further right now.'

His gaze dropped insolently to her breasts where they rose and fell with her jagged breath under her dress and Orla hissed, 'You're disgusting.' But to her chagrin it came out without much conviction. More as a breathless entreaty.

Antonio stood tall again and his gaze turned cool. 'Run along back to your hotel, Orla. I'll be in touch when I'm good and ready.'

Antonio watched Orla's exquisite face suffuse with colour at his blatantly patronising tone. But to give her credit, she controlled her temper and merely turned on her heel and stalked out of the room, that vibrant silken fall of hair like a splash of fire against the green.

When she was gone, Antonio couldn't relax. She filled his mind's eye. She'd been undone just now, before she'd turned to go. Clothes creased, hair down, eyes huge and glittering. Mouth swollen. And it had been the hardest thing in the world to taunt her, but making her eyes flash venom at him had been the only thing stopping him from smashing the table aside between them, locking the door and putting her back on the desk to finish what they'd started.

If her ringing phone hadn't interrupted them, he'd been about to free his aching erection, slide aside her panties and thrust so deep into her he would have seen nirvana. And she'd been with him all the way, about to beg him for it. Despite her words last week that she wouldn't even if he were the last man on the planet. It was cold comfort now.

Antonio went to the window and looked out. For the

past decade of his life he'd lived by a strict code. A code that had saved his life and the lives of many others over and over again. But as soon as that red-haired siren came within a mile radius of him, that code went out the window and he was reduced to some primeval being. Snarling, full of craven base desires. Inarticulate. Insulting. Less than a gentleman. Indeed, he deserved that accusation. The Legion had made him rough. It had broken him down and rebuilt him and along the way he'd lost the smooth veneer that a life of privilege had given him.

However, he could still fake it when he needed to. But not with *her*.

This made him nervous. Because the control he wielded in his life now was fragile on many levels. In many ways he was still recuperating from things that he would never breathe a word of to a living soul. They were things that he would take to his grave.

After the horrors he'd witnessed while in the Legion, Antonio had resigned himself not so much to living, as surviving. And not one thing till now had caused him to believe that he could expect anything else. Not one thing…till Orla Kennedy had walked into that bar last week and breathed light and life into some dark part of him.

Sighing heavily, Antonio went and sat back down and resisted the urge to call his therapist, who had brought him back from the brink of madness. His therapist might be able to help untangle the knots of his mind and psyche but only one person could help untangle the knots in his body.

*'Run along back to your hotel, Orla.'* Orla shook her head and fumed again at the way Antonio had all but

patted her on the backside to help her *run along*. After kissing her so senseless that she'd been ready to have sex with him on his office table!

She'd been fuming for three days now. Her staff had been keeping a wide berth when they saw her coming. Even Tom, their solicitor, had left her alone after Orla had told him succinctly, 'He'll give us what we want and that's as far as I'm prepared to discuss it right now.'

Antonio Chatsfield would give them what they wanted because she was right about their motives for wanting to buy out the Kennedy Group. He just hated that she'd figured it out.

Orla's phone beeped with a text message and she turned from where she'd been looking broodingly out of her office window to pick it up. It was an unidentified number and the message read: I'm in your hotel. A.

Immediately her heart rate increased and her legs went wobbly. She cursed. And then castigated herself. This was one of the conditions, wasn't it? She'd asked him here after all.

Angry at the physical reaction he provoked so effortlessly, she punched back, Where?

Two seconds later: Come find me.

Fuming even more now that he was playing games, Orla clutched her phone in her hand and left her office, steam practically coming out of her ears.

When she reached the grand marble lobby it was busy with people checking in and out. Normally this would have made her feel satisfied inside; now she didn't even notice.

Eventually she spotted him, sitting in one of the antique high-backed chairs around the focal featured fireplace, reading the distinctive pink *Financial Times*. She walked over and stopped in front of him, arms crossed, tapping her foot impatiently. When he didn't take the paper down to acknowledge her, she cleared her throat loudly.

With a supreme nonchalance that grated along her nerves, he deigned to lower his paper and Orla had to keep her eyes up, resisting the urge to take in that glorious physique. She could see that he was in a three-piece suit, complete with tie. Oozing urbanity. When she knew just how crude he could be. Again that thought didn't disgust her; it excited her. She was pathetic.

He folded the paper and stood up, easily dwarfing Orla in spite of her three-inch heels. Remembering all too well his patronising send-off the other day, she said frigidly, 'I'm afraid I'm rather busy at the moment, but I can arrange for one of our managers to show you around.'

Just then one of the receptionists hurried over, wreathed in smiles, eyes sparkling. She had a key card in her hand. 'I have your room key, Mr Chatsfield. Sorry to keep you waiting. Your bags have already been delivered to the suite. If you'd like to follow me I can show you to the room personally.'

Orla's mouth dropped open as she looked from Kelly, whom she now recognised as one of the trainee receptionists, to Antonio, who was smiling with all the mega-wattage and charisma of a movie star.

Before she could get a word out, Antonio said with smooth charm, 'Thank you so much, Kelly, but your lovely owner here, Miss Kennedy, has offered to do just that.'

With almost palpable reluctance Kelly handed the room key over to Orla, who vowed to have a word with the young trainee about how to behave with their customers. No matter *how* gorgeous or alluring they might be. Her desire to chastise the girl had nothing to do with the way Antonio had smiled so sexily just now. Nothing at all.

Orla stalked away from Antonio across the marble floor of the distinctive and classic foyer, her heels sounding like angry staccato bullets on the floor, not looking to see if he was following.

She pressed for the lift and tensed minutely when she felt Antonio's much larger presence close to her back. Her skin prickled and tightened. Her nipples peaked.

The lift doors opened and she stepped in. Followed by Antonio. They were the only people to get in. The doors closed and Orla folded her arms and rounded on him. 'What the hell do you think you're doing?'

Antonio leant back against the mirrored lift wall and tried to curb the predictable and annoying surge of desire. Orla was wearing a dark blue silk shirt that made her eyes seem darker, and a black pencil skirt. Court shoes. Hair down and sleek. She looked like a million other women in this city—cool, efficient, successful. But she was also nothing like those other women. He realised now that she had an earthy sensuality hidden underneath those impeccable clothes. It had called to him the moment he'd laid eyes on her. She also had an endearing edge of vulnerability that she tried to disguise with that uber-efficient career-woman exterior.

Antonio didn't welcome these insights. This woman was an obstacle to making his sister happy. That was all.

It didn't help that the last time they'd shared a lift, she'd exposed herself to him on his command. A vision of that small but plump and pert pale breast filled his mind now and his gaze tracked automatically to her chest, but Orla's arms were clamped furiously over any evidence of his effect on her.

Angry with himself now for his own lack of control when for the past decade his life had been the byword in control, even under the worst of conditions, Antonio said, 'Floor eight please. I'm in the penthouse.'

He also cursed himself silently for having thought it would be a good idea to move into the Kennedy hotel.

Orla's mouth was a thin line of displeasure. Clearly she hated the idea too. 'The buttons are on your side of the lift. I'm not a lift attendant.'

Antonio disguised a grimace and pressed the appropriate button. What was it about this woman that reduced him so effortlessly to some kind of Cro-Magnon man?

Orla was all but tapping a foot again as the lift ascended swiftly and silently. 'Well?'

Antonio made a supreme effort to be normal. He kept his eyes on hers. 'You did ask me to come and see how things were run. That's exactly what I'm doing.'

The lift came to a halt. The doors slid open. People were waiting outside and Orla's open mouth closed as she pasted a bright smile on her face and stepped out. Antonio followed. She was stalking down the hall to a door at the end. Vaguely Antonio took in the details of pleasant furnishings, muted classic colours. But he was far more interested in the sway of Orla's shapely bottom in that tight skirt.

She had opened the door to the suite and was holding it for him, and hating every second by the look on her face. He walked in and her scent tickled his nostrils. Fresh but with a hint of earthy muskiness. Like her. All cool and collected on the outside, but hiding an inner tigress.

He walked in and surveyed the lavish spacious penthouse suite, complete with a terrace patio. It wasn't as obviously luxurious as the Chatsfield but something about its classic simplicity appealed to him. He heard her cool voice behind him. 'You know very well that I did not mean that you should come and stay here.'

Antonio curbed his own temper and turned to face her. Still those arms crossed over her chest. He could see a hint of cleavage now though, in the V of that silk material. He gritted his teeth to control his body.

'If this is how you treat all your guests, then it's no wonder your business is going down the tubes.'

She flushed at that and Antonio had the bizarre urge to apologise. He noticed again that she looked tired. He knew she was holding the fort as her father hadn't yet returned from his Asia trip.

Smiling sweetly now, sweetly enough for something to kick in Antonio's gut, she said, 'Don't worry, you're getting very special personal treatment. If you would be so kind as to let me know how long you'll be staying we will, of course, ensure that your visit is as pleasant as possible.'

Antonio wanted to scowl at her seasoned impersonal managerial patter. 'I'm playing it by ear.'

She flushed again, deeper this time, but obviously bit back whatever she really wanted to say. 'If you'll excuse me, I have appointments to attend to. I'll send up one of my junior managers to give you a tour.'

Antonio rejected that outright. 'Orla…' he said warningly.

She turned from where she'd been walking back to the door. Her eyes flashed and there was steel in her tone. 'Don't push it, Chatsfield.' And then she turned and left the suite and Antonio had to admit to a grudging rise of respect. He wasn't used to people standing up to him.

He went to the French doors and opened them and walked out to the patio, feeling constricted. He had to battle this feeling on a regular basis, still not fully used to being back in a bustling metropolis. He had to get it together where Orla Kennedy was concerned. He put his hands on the stone wall, and looked out over the famous London skyline, soaring into the sunshine.

He'd once had a reputation for being charming and urbane. Along with being a renowned playboy. He'd lived hard and worked hard, intent on keeping his family together, before all his efforts had proved futile. Even then, he'd still been whole—before he'd seen the worst of humanity and had become twisted and blackened inside along the way.

His hands tightened on the stone. Surely there was a sliver of that man left inside him? He smiled grimly. He'd drawn on it the other night when he'd seduced a beautiful sexy stranger in a bar. Maybe it wasn't so far beneath the surface after all…. He needed to change tactics with Orla and the tactics he envisaged were going to be every bit as low-down and dirty as anything he'd done as a soldier, but infinitely more personally pleasurable.

Orla was tired. She'd spent the whole day yesterday reeling from the shock of having Antonio Chatsfield check into the hotel, terrified he'd appear around a corner at any moment. But there had been no sign of him. One of the junior managers had told her that they'd helped him to set up an office space in the suite, so clearly he was working.

And she'd just managed to get through another day without seeing him. Orla didn't like to admit that her primary emotion wasn't relief. It was something far more ambiguous.

Already envisaging taking off her shoes and running a hot bath with lots of bubbles, Orla walked into her office and came to a complete standstill. Antonio Chatsfield was behind her desk, sitting in her chair, reading the weekly report she hadn't yet had time to read herself, with his feet propped up on her desk, crossed at the ankle.

He didn't even look up, just said, 'Your figures aren't that bad, you know, for a business that's on its way under.'

Orla walked in and reached across her desk to pluck the report out of Antonio's fingers. He appeared completely unperturbed. Dressed in an open-necked shirt and dark trousers, the smart clothes still couldn't hide his virile potency.

Orla had been feeling weary. Now she was zinging with energy. She gritted her teeth and forced herself to stay calm. 'Can I help you? I trust you're settling in well?'

Antonio brought his feet down and sat up straight. 'Your staff have been most solicitous…no doubt instructed well by you.'

Orla counted to ten and said evenly, 'We treat everyone here the same, Antonio, from the person staying in the budget single room to the VIP guest in the penthouse.'

Antonio stood up and immediately Orla's breath got choppier.

'Very commendable.' His voice held no mockery but Orla stared at him suspiciously. She felt self-conscious even though she was dressed smartly in a cream shirt dress, cinched in with a wide leather belt, and nude heels. Hair pulled back into a low ponytail.

Antonio put his hands in his pockets and regarded her for a moment until Orla started to get hot and said tetchily, 'What is it? Have I got dirt on my face?'

Antonio's voice sounded slightly rough around the edges. 'You could pass for twenty-one.'

Heat zinged through Orla's pelvis at the lazy sensual look in his eyes, making her grow damp between her legs. She cursed herself and said briskly, 'Well, I'm a long way off twenty-one. Nine years to be precise. Now if you don't mind, it's been a long day and I still have work to do.'

It was a white lie but she wanted this man who was too big, too masculine, *too much*, out of her space before he saw how brittle he made her feel. He moved around her desk into the office and that only made Orla feel even more tetchy. And then with absolutely no warning, he delivered the bombshell.

'I'd like to buy you dinner tonight.'

For a second Orla couldn't compute Antonio's words. And then she parroted back, 'Dinner? Tonight?'

He crossed his arms across his massive chest, drawing Orla's helpless gaze to the bunching of his biceps under the material of his shirt.

'Yes…it's a common concept—a social event indulged in by people who wish to spend time together over food.'

Orla's gaze lifted and clashed with a very dark one. She could see humour dancing in the depths and her belly swooped dangerously. Reminding her of the other night. Reminding her of the stranger who had seduced her so easily.

She opened her mouth to say something acerbic but Antonio cut her off, saying silkily, 'Don't waste your breath, Orla. I checked your diary and you've nothing on. I've booked a table at the Kilkenny restaurant downstairs for 8:00 p.m. Don't be late.'

And with that, he walked out, leaving his scent in the air, exotic and spicy. *Male.* Orla's hands curled to fists and she wondered helplessly just what it was about him that made her feel so threatened?

Her inner conscience laughed itself silly. Where did she start? He'd threatened her equilibrium as soon as she'd laid eyes on him. But she'd ignored that to jump into bed with him within an hour of meeting him.

This man, who was her adversary, had seen her at her absolute worst. Behaving so out of character that it made her feel ill to think about it. But what was even worse—it hadn't been just a clinical emotionless one-night stand, not that she'd even know what that felt like. Not for her anyway. She still remembered all too well those raw feelings she'd had the next morning. The raw feelings she'd had when he'd joined their bodies.

She still remembered the assertion that she'd never felt so intimate with another person...when he'd been a complete stranger! And the regret she'd felt walking away. Not even knowing his real name.

Orla's mouth thinned and she walked around her desk and sat into her chair, which felt bigger, as if he'd stretched it with his masculine bulk. Well, fate had laughed in her face at *that* feeling of regret. Fate had given her precisely four hours of believing she was still in control of her life after behaving like a lust-obsessed groupie.

She'd known what lay ahead of her in terms of negotiating this takeover by the Chatsfields. And that it was going to be an uphill struggle at the best of times, because it was only for the fact that it suited the Chatsfields to buy them out that this deal was even being discussed. There was every possibility they'd start to think it wasn't worth the trouble and walk away. And Orla was doing nothing to help that from happening. The fact that Antonio Chatsfield, the architect behind the deal, was the man who'd seen her at her most wanton and uninhibited had turned this from an uphill struggle to a nearly impossible one.

That was why he made her feel so threatened. And that was just for starters. And there was no way that she had a choice about dinner. Sighing deeply, Orla relegated the image of a relaxing bath to the back of her head. For as long as Antonio Chatsfield was in her life there would be no relaxing.

'Good evening, Miss Kennedy. Your guest is waiting for you.'

'Thank you, Brendan.' Orla acknowledged their maître d' and cursed the fact that she already felt breathless as she made her way across the dining room of the Michelin-starred Kilkenny restaurant. One of the reasons why their London hotel in particular was so attractive to the Chatsfields.

The lighting was dim in the wood-panelled dining room that had a library feel. Its discreet booths and tables attracted politicians, writers, artists, A-listers escaping the paparazzi and a general moneyed exclusive clientele, and Orla couldn't help but be proud of it now. It was a testament to her father's hard work and dedication.

Suddenly Orla felt very emotional to think of all of this being taken out of their hands and fought it down as she came closer and closer to the booth table at the back wall where she could see a familiar broad-shouldered figure. She cursed Antonio for picking such a private spot. She'd prefer a table right in the middle of the restaurant.

Instinctively she smoothed down her midnight-blue silk dress. It was knee-length. Completely demure—long-sleeved, with buttons running from waist to neck, not a peephole in sight.

She'd teamed it with matching slingback heels and a small silver clutch bag. She'd twisted her hair up in a chignon, determined not to give Antonio the impression that this dinner was about anything but business. Even if treacherous nerves that would be more appropriate if she were going on a date were jumping around in her belly.

# CHAPTER FIVE

ANTONIO SAW ORLA approach him, winding through the tables with that innate grace he'd noticed when he'd first seen her. He also saw the firm set of her jaw and the hard line of her mouth. Her dress sent out serious Sunday-school teacher vibes but was all the more sexy because of that.

And clearly Orla believed she was sending out the message she wanted to because her chin had a definite hitch to it that screamed, *I'm here for business only*, as she finally arrived and Antonio stood automatically to greet her.

She slid into the booth, making sure to stay firmly on the opposite side to Antonio. Eyes sliding away from his. Taking the menu being offered by the waiter who had sprung into action as soon as she'd sat down.

Orla smiled warmly at him. 'Thank you, Thomas. How's your mother doing?'

The young man blushed. 'She's grand, Miss Kennedy. She'll be heading home from the hospital next week and please God that'll be the last of the treatments, thanks to you and your father.'

'I'm glad. It's been a tough time.'

The man murmured something and ducked away to

let them peruse the menus. Antonio found that he was slightly stunned after watching that little interplay. He felt something dark grip him inside to see how Orla's warm smile had faded as soon as the man had left. As soon as she'd smiled at the man Antonio had felt like grabbing him by the scruff of the neck.

Goaded by that spiky darkness, Antonio prompted with a drawl, 'Good evening to you too.'

He saw her hands tense on the big leather menu and something in him got hotter. Not as unaffected as she'd like to appear. She lifted those long-lashed dark blue eyes to his. 'Good evening.'

Antonio inclined his head and tried to tamp down on the surge of lust in his blood. 'You know the waiter well?'

Orla nodded her head, her eyes losing that icy coolness for a second as if she couldn't help herself. Her voice was husky. 'Yes, his mother is from where my family are from in the west of Ireland. She's worked for us for years in the accounts office but she's been battling cancer for the past few months. Thankfully it would appear as if the treatment is working....'

Antonio thought of something the man had said and asked curiously, 'Has your family been paying for the treatment?'

Orla immediately flushed and sounded defensive. 'Most of it has been covered by the NHS.... We've just helped out along the way.'

Something tightened inside Antonio at this evidence of caring for their staff. If there was one incident like this, how many more were there? Draining the business of valuable finances?

As if reading his mind, Orla said, 'This was a special case—they're personal friends of my father's.'

Antonio put down his menu and arched a brow. 'And what about the special case of the eighty-year-old concierge who I noticed has to be shadowed at all times by a younger colleague presumably because he's about to keel over dead?'

Two spots of colour burned in her cheeks. 'He's training them in. He's been with this hotel from the very start. He's an institution. Loyal guests come back just to see Lawrence. He retired officially years ago but this is all he knows, so as long as he's fit to work and wants to, we see no reason to let him go.'

Antonio had to admit that he'd had quite an entertaining conversation with the old man today, finding him to be surprisingly alert and knowledgable. Still… it was hardly best practice hiring old-age pensioners to be at the front of house.

Orla put down her menu, her voice tight and eyes flashing. 'I'm not going to stay here and listen to you list off—'

Immediately Antonio reacted. He reached across and stopped Orla with a hand on her wrist. Her pulse was throbbing fast against her skin. Cursing himself for losing sight of his game plan so quickly, Antonio said, 'I'm sorry, OK? Let's call a truce. No more talk of work, at least during dinner.'

*Let's call a truce.*

Orla could feel her pulse beating like a caged bird against Antonio's hand. Loath to let him see how much he affected her, she pulled free. The thought of a truce was almost as terrifying as the thought of the takeover but she had no choice.

'Fine.' And she took the menu up again quickly, seeing nothing of the words. Only feeling her heart thumping and her skin getting hot. He disturbed her so effortlessly and she hated it.

The waiter came back and Orla asked for the special; Antonio asked for the Irish beef steak, a signature dish of the restaurant.

She finally lowered her menu and Antonio looked at her. 'Wine?'

Acting on a reflex to deny that this was anything remotely like a date, she shook her head quickly and said, 'Not for me, thanks. I'll stick to sparkling water.' Even though right now she felt as if she could do with a mammoth glass of wine.

She looked to the waiter and smiled at him again, glad of the dilution of energy swirling between her and Antonio. When Antonio had given a wine order and she glanced at him, he was almost scowling at her, eyes fixated on her mouth.

And then his gaze moved up and his expression transformed into something far more benign, so quickly that she might have imagined that scowl or his eyes on her lips. Damn her pulse. It wouldn't calm down.

Another waiter returned almost immediately with wine, and water for Orla. She watched as Antonio took his time tasting the wine. There was something so inherently sensual about the way he did it that her limbs turned to liquid and she thought she might just slide under the table altogether.

Grabbing on to the table edge as much to root her in the room as anything else, she watched as Antonio nodded to the sommelier. When the woman had left, he stared at her and arched a brow. He lifted the bottle. 'Are you sure you won't have a little? It's good.'

Orla knew it was good; it was one of the wines she'd

chosen for their cellar herself. She was about to open her mouth and say something frigid, again, but suddenly it felt like too much of an effort and a voice inside berated her. *Truce.* Giving in, she even smiled minutely and held up her glass. 'OK then, just a small bit.'

Antonio looked as if he was repressing a smile too, and something light cut through the tension. They both took a sip of wine and Antonio said, 'I know the owner of this vineyard.'

Her eyes widened. 'The owner of the Piacenza vineyard? I didn't think anyone knew his identity.'

Antonio inclined his head. 'He's allowed his privacy. But they grow some fantastic local varietals. Malvasia, Barbera, along with some merlot and pinot noir.'

'How do you know so much about wine?' Orla was intrigued.

'I did a master of wine course in my early twenties.... I came across the vineyard near Milan at the time.'

Orla's eyes nearly boggled out of her head. 'You're a master of wine?'

Antonio looked mildly sheepish. 'Yes.'

Orla whistled softly. 'That's some achievement. There's only a few hundred in the world.'

Antonio mocked, 'Careful now. You sound almost approving.'

Orla twirled her wine glass in her hands and then looked at him, mocking back, 'I had you down as a meathead ex-soldier. So how does a master of wine end up in the French Foreign Legion and survive?'

Immediately Antonio's eyes narrowed on her and the air cooled. 'Been doing your homework?'

Orla shrugged lightly, belying her sense of intimidation. 'It's common knowledge you went to the Legion.'

She glanced at him; his eyes had darkened. She widened hers against the tremor in the region of her gut. 'What? I thought we'd called a truce? I'm merely trying to make conversation.'

A voice chided her, *Way to go with keeping to truce-appropriate topics.*

After a long moment Antonio shrugged one broad shoulder. Now he was avoiding her eye. Gazing into his wine. 'I joined when I was twenty-five.'

Curious now, Orla said, 'Why not earlier? Surely twenty-five is relatively old to join an army?'

Antonio's face was expressionless as he looked at her. 'I wasn't in a position to earlier. I had my family to think about.'

Orla pushed aside the urge to ask him to elaborate on what he meant by that and admitted, 'I know nothing about it apart from the myths and legends…the fact that it's secretive and the training is brutal. That you have to give up your name and passport.'

Antonio took a sip of wine and his mouth tipped up on one corner, but Orla's gaze was distracted momentarily by the strong bronzed column of his throat. She had the sudden desire to flick her tongue there, tasting him.

'That's about as much as I knew before I went in,' he admitted. 'I walked in the gate at Fort de Nogent in Paris, handed in my passport and didn't get it back for seven years.'

A shiver went through Orla. 'I can't imagine just handing yourself over to something like that.'

Antonio's expression was enigmatic. 'And yet don't we do it every day? Haven't you given yourself over to your career, to your family business?'

Immediately feeling defensive, Orla blustered, 'That's different!'

'How?' Antonio just asked. 'Because you're not leaving your home, changing identity?'

'Did you have to change your identity?' Orla was referring to the fact that when someone joined the Legion, they had to give up their own name and take on another, usually given to them by the Legion.

Antonio's mouth firmed for a moment as if he resented her diverting the conversation away again. He nodded. 'Yes, but after a period of time you can resume your own identity again. It's not as strict as it used to be.'

'And did you take your name back?'

He shook his head after a long moment. His face was cast in shadows. Her voice husky, Orla asked, 'Why not? Who were you?'

Antonio answered with steel in his tone. 'Someone else.'

Just then they were interrupted by the waiter returning with starters. Orla felt slightly disorientated and was more fascinated than she liked to admit to about Antonio's experiences in the Legion. But before she could probe any further he asked a question of his own.

'So, how about you? Were you born in one of those suits you like to wear with your hair all neat and tidy?'

Orla scowled at him and he smiled, shameless. Her belly tightened with a spasm of lust. Somewhere along the way she was losing sight of what this dinner was; the lines were getting blurred. She took a bite of her asparagus starter and tried to control herself.

When she was able to she answered impulsively, wanting to wipe the smug look off Antonio's face. 'Actually, if you must know I was a tearaway tomboy for the first nine years of my life. I hated dresses. Couldn't stand being indoors. I had more scrapes and bruises than any boy I knew, much to the disgust of my mother....'

Antonio put down his fork. 'What happened when you were nine?'

Orla stared at him and realised what she'd just said. Cold horror flooded her because she'd been nine when she'd overheard that conversation of her father's and had changed overnight. Feeling very exposed now, she shrugged and avoided his eye. 'I guess I turned into a girl.'

Antonio's deep voice came like a caress. 'Something happened. No one changes overnight.'

Orla looked at him, but he just looked back at her and raised a brow. Feeling inordinately threatened, she finally admitted, 'It was an overnight decision actually, but it came about because of something I overheard.'

With the utmost reluctance, Orla described overhearing her father talking and her resolve to be there for him. To shoulder the responsibility of being his only heir.

'The fact is,' Orla pointed out before Antonio could say anything, 'I loved it. I used to sit in on his meetings and take notes, pretending to be his secretary. And then as I got older, I took notes for real.'

Antonio sat back a little, those enigmatic eyes unreadable. 'What about your mother?'

Orla tensed and pushed away her starter plate. She avoided Antonio's eye. 'My mother...just isn't really interested in the business side of things. She used to be though, when I was small. I'd see her and my father working late, going over figures, deciding on interior decoration...which hotel to invest in next.

'But then…' Orla shrugged and tailed off, not wanting to reveal how her mother had been seduced by their wealth as it had grown, to the point where that was all she cared about now.

To her relief a waiter came and cleared their starters, cutting her off. When they were alone again Antonio asked, 'Do you have a home in London?'

Orla breathed a small sigh of relief that he wasn't going to pursue the last topic of conversation. She shook her head and felt a familiar pang. 'No, I live here at the hotel. We've always lived in the hotels…one or other of them. The one here in London for the past twenty years, since it was opened.'

'You've always lived in your hotels?'

She nodded again. 'Didn't you?'

He shook his head. 'We have a family home outside London. We grew up there…although we did run riot around the hotel here all our lives. Drove our parents crazy, of course.'

Orla felt wistful and heard herself admitting, 'I missed not having siblings.'

Antonio's expression became enigmatic again. 'I had too many and you had none. We're never happy, are we?'

An efficient waiter reappeared with their main courses and Orla smiled her thanks. Antonio's comment about never being happy reverberated inside her.

Orla speared some lamb. It was succulent and gorgeous but her taste buds had suddenly dried up. Their conversation felt far too…easy, yet with a delicious edge of tension.

They concentrated on their food for a few minutes and a ridiculous ripple of pride went through Orla when

Antonio commented that the steak was one of the best he'd ever tasted.

After the brief lull, almost against her will Orla found herself blurting into the silence, 'I always wanted a house. A family home. I was so envious of my friends when I'd go back to their houses. That they could shut the front door and not have to deal with hundreds of strangers right outside their door.'

Embarrassed now, Orla flushed and avoided Antonio's gaze. 'Don't get me wrong. I know how lucky I was—I had an incredibly privileged upbringing. But sometimes…I wished that I had my own space. That when I came back to my bedroom after school the bed wouldn't be turned down with a sweet on the pillow and all my things tidied away.'

Antonio said nothing for a moment and then, 'We might have had a home…but we were cut off from the outside world to a large extent. Shuttled from exclusive boarding schools back to a huge bleak house filled with nannies and housekeepers. Our parents were invariably in one of the hotels…. We were pretty much left to our own devices and then our mother left when I was fifteen.'

Orla felt a pang near her heart. Everyone knew the story of Liliana Chatsfield walking out on her family all those years ago only to vanish into thin air, leaving behind a baby and her six older children. That was when the gilt edges had started crumbling from the Chatsfield empire.

As much as her own mother drove her to distraction now, she'd been there for Orla her whole life.

'That must have been rough. And you never saw her again?'

Antonio wiped at his mouth with a linen napkin and shook his head quickly. Orla had the distinct feeling that he wasn't about to elaborate on that part of his life. She had a memory flash at that moment of being about eighteen or nineteen and seeing Antonio splashed all over the tabloids emerging from a nightclub with a bevy of semi-naked beauties.

She could remember how devilishly gorgeous he'd been, but far younger and more innocent looking than the man in front of her now. Which was why she hadn't recognised him. That had been just before he'd disappeared off the scene completely and then one by one the other Chatsfields had grown up and started to take his place in the papers with regularity.

As recently as a few weeks before, his youngest sister, Cara, who was stunning and irrepressible, had been in the headlines for doing something debauched. Orla found herself wondering, what must it have been like for him to take on the burden of responsibility so young? Much like herself.

She'd never in a million years have felt like she'd have anything in common with a privileged Chatsfield. The revelation was uncomfortable.

'I presume you didn't see your sisters and brothers much since you went away?'

Antonio didn't move a muscle, but Orla could sense him tensing. He took his wine glass in his big hand and rolled it, making the rich red liquid swirl hypnotically.

'No,' he answered finally. 'I didn't. They were all pretty much grown up when I left, except for the twins, Orsino and Lucca, who were finishing school, and Cara, who was ten.'

His mouth tightened to a bitter line. 'But as my father pointed out to me, *he* was their father not me. Even though it only suited him to be a father every now and then. I had a fight with him on a day when evidently it had suited him.'

Orla felt her way. 'A fight?'

Antonio nodded curtly. 'About my brother Nicolo. He'd been badly scarred in a fire when he was thirteen. I was worried about him because he'd gone from being a hellraiser to living as a recluse. I knew that he'd never really come to terms with what had happened but he didn't want to hear it from me.'

Orla's chest grew tight at the thought of Antonio as a young man trying his best to be a parent to his brothers and sisters. She wanted to ask him more but just then their waiter came and took plates away and Orla was shocked to see that she'd practically shared the bottle of wine with Antonio in the end.

She was also more than a little stunned by that last conversation. They'd deviated way off the tracks. So much for her keeping things cool and businesslike. She'd been all but hanging off his every word like some lovesick teenager. Quickly she asked for coffee, wanting to clear her head a little. Antonio Chatsfield was proving to be far more interesting and deep than she would have ever given him credit for.

When their coffees had been delivered, Orla was determined to bring things back onto more familiar ground. 'So why come back now to do this? Be part of a takeover bid?'

Antonio's eyes flashed. 'I thought we were going to avoid contentious subjects?'

Orla lifted her chin.

Mock-sadly, Antonio replied to her silence. 'The truce was nice while it lasted.'

He took a sip of coffee and then put his cup down. 'I came home to do this now for my sister Lucilla. When I left home, she shouldered the burden of caring for our siblings and also running the business. She's asked me to look after this one thing for her...so I am.'

He speared Orla with a dark look. 'If you're trying to figure out how soon I'll be gone again, Orla, don't waste your time. You have my undivided attention until we become the new owners of the Kennedy Group. And it will happen...sooner or later.'

Orla's hand tightened on her coffee cup so much that she had to relax for fear of breaking it. She couldn't escape that compelling gaze. There was steel in Antonio's tone.

The depth of his loyalty to his sister was tangible and after what he'd just told her she could well imagine how strong a bond had been forged after their mother had left. She was up against blood ties, blood loyalty. And yet, so was he. She had just as much riding on this deal as he had for the sake of *her* family.

Suddenly feeling as sober as a judge despite the wine, and also disturbingly exposed to hear Antonio lay out his loyalty to his sister so starkly, Orla forced herself to finish her coffee and wiped her mouth.

She injected as much lightness into her voice as she could muster. 'I think I'll retire. It's been a long day and we have a convention arriving tomorrow, early.'

Antonio smiled and it looked like a shark's smile in the soft light. No less threatening. Orla felt cold. She couldn't believe she'd been intimate with this man only a few nights ago.

'I'll see you up to your room.'

Orla opened her mouth and saw the stern set of Antonio's mouth and jaw. It was futile to argue.

'Fine,' she replied tightly, 'knock yourself out.'

They stood up and Antonio let Orla precede him out of the booth. He noted that her cheeks were flushed. From the wine? Or from the desire-saturated air that swirled around them? Or from the realisation that she was fighting a losing battle to keep control of her family business?

To his surprise, Antonio felt a pang at that. He couldn't help but acknowledge how hard Orla worked. He'd observed her over the past couple of days when she'd been unaware. She'd been tireless. Up at dawn, to bed late at night. Unfailingly polite and warm to guests and staff alike. In fact, it was a kind of dedication and service that he knew was lacking in their hotel business, mainly because of its size and success.

The Kennedy Group clearly still had that very personal touch. And Antonio had to admit that it had to do with the fabled Irish charm too. He'd watched Orla switch it on, exactly as she had with that waiter earlier. And it was completely sincere. The guests loved it. And the staff were steadfastly loyal. He'd been given the gimlet eye by more than a few as he'd made his rounds, checking things out.

Orla walked in front of him through the restaurant now, hips swaying in her silk dress. The back of her neck looked intensely vulnerable with her hair up and he had to fight the urge to tug it down so that it feathered across her shoulders as it had done the other night. Which felt like an aeon ago. When they'd been different people. Strangers. Lovers.

The lobby area was quiet. Orla went to the reception desk to check in with the staff before calling out goodnight as she made her way to where Antonio waited at the lifts. He was propped against the wall, hands in his pockets.

He could see as she approached that she got tenser. Her shoulders a stiff line. He pressed the button for the lift and the doors opened smoothly. Stepping in, he looked at her questioningly, and after a taut moment, a silent battle of wills, she said, 'Floor five. Please.'

The doors slid shut again and she obviously noted that he didn't push the button for his own floor. She looked very petite in the small space and Antonio was automatically thinking of how she'd exposed herself to him that night. And then afterwards…how tight she'd been. How responsive. Desire surged and he hoped she wouldn't glance down right now.

As if she was battling with the same carnal memories, she blurted out, 'You don't have to walk me all the way to my door. We're not in a dodgy street, for heaven's sake.'

Antonio just stared at her and couldn't control the intense flare of heat in his groin. Her hair was so bright against this backdrop, vivid red. Her skin so pale. Eyes so blue. He wanted her with a hunger he'd never experienced before. Not even after months of celibacy in the army; he hadn't indulged while he'd been on active service, preferring to wait until he was on leave. As a result of that Antonio prided himself on his ability to maintain control…not any more.

Forcing himself to not sound as desperate for her as he felt, he drawled, 'I insist. I want to prove to you that I can be a gentleman, Orla.'

He almost felt sorry for her when she said far too fervently, 'I believe you. Really.'

But then the doors opened and Antonio indicated for her to get out. He saw her jaw clench, but then she stepped out and he followed. Her room was at the end of the corridor. She put her key card in the door and it opened. She turned around immediately and he could see the pulse beating at the base of her neck. Frantic. He remembered how her pulse had felt under his hand earlier and his own sped up in response.

'OK, thank you. This is me.'

He knew she was aiming for jocular but it came out forced and something resonated deep inside him. Telling himself this was just all part of the game plan to unsettle this woman, he drawled, 'Aren't you going to invite me in?'

'Certainly not.'

Antonio had to smile at Orla's frigid tone as he pointed out dryly, 'Need I remind you that you don't have to put on the scandalised-virgin act?'

She spat out now, her cheeks high with colour, 'We both know neither of us are virgins.'

Antonio's body tightened. And yet he'd guess that she hadn't been very experienced at all. In spite of her bravado that night.

He was actually about to admit defeat and step back and leave her when she opened the door wider and said huffily, 'For heaven's sake, you can satisfy yourself that there are no intruders and then leave....'

Antonio's body reacted, blood leaping, keeping his

body aroused, hard. She stood back and he walked in. Immediately a faintly exotic scent assailed his nostrils, unlike the usual hotel scent. It was her scent, and as he walked into the suite of rooms he had to stop his jaw from falling open.

She had obviously completely redecorated the suite to suit her tastes. *To create the home she spoke of missing out on?* His chest tightened. Everything was soothing, calming—in tones of off-white. A big comfortable couch and low table with two armchairs. A state-of-the-art TV and music system. Beautiful watercolour paintings on the walls. It had a visceral effect on him, tugging on some deep echo within himself of a long-forgotten desire for his own space and...*peace.*

Everything was pristine, neat and tidy. Bookshelves set up against one wall, but he could see that they were temporary and didn't like how that made something protective rise up within him.

He found himself being drawn to one of the watercolours on the wall. It featured a stunning wild landscape/seascape in greens and blues. He sensed Orla's presence beside him, her unique scent, mirroring that of the room.

Her voice was husky, tugging on his nerve endings. Making them sensitive. 'That's Slea Head in Kerry, near where we come from. In the west of Ireland.'

Antonio didn't like to admit how something in the picture called to the wildness he'd felt inside him for a long time.

Something was shifting. Things weren't so cut and dried. Yes, he wanted to seduce this woman and get her to comply with his demands for his sister's benefit, and apart from that he wanted her with a hunger like no other. But now…it was as if he was getting a glimpse into her soul. And it made him feel disorientated.

Orla felt like screaming into the deafening silence as Antonio gazed intently at the painting as if he were at a gallery and not standing in her very private rooms. *Say something!* She berated herself for letting him come in. She was normally fanatical about her privacy, but when he'd been lounging in her doorway looking so big and *sexy*…something inside her had weakened. Something wild and wanton had risen. Like the other night.

She never even allowed the hotel staff to come into this suite of rooms, cleaning them herself—she had that phobia of someone rearranging things while she was out.

The conversation they'd just had over dinner had made something indefinable change within her though. Some defence she'd been clinging to was shakier, weaker. Pathetically, she'd gone from coldly declaring, *No*, to standing aside to let him in within seconds. This man who threatened her on so many levels.

Orla felt completely exposed and vulnerable now. She folded her arms across her chest. Her voice was tight. 'I think we can assume I'm safe now.'

Antonio's big body went still. He slowly turned around to face her, gazed down at her. Orla stopped breathing and went hot all over. He was so big.

He was also the epitome of elegant masculinity in his dark suit and light grey open-necked shirt. On the surface. But just below that, Orla sensed the danger oozing from every gorgeous pore. He really looked about as urbane as a wild panther prowling the city streets.

She went distinctly wobbly as he closed the distance

between them. He lifted his hands and she only realised what he was doing when she felt her hair fall down around her shoulders. Pinprick needles of sensations exploded all over her body.

Ineffectually she put up her hands. 'Wait, what are you doing?'

Antonio's eyes glittered darkly. Orla saw him casually throw the pin that had been holding her hair up onto a nearby chair.

'What I *want* to do,' he said in that deep rough voice, 'is make love to you. Because you've been torturing me for days. Because I don't think I can walk out that door again without touching you first....'

His face tightened. 'But if you don't want this, say it now, Orla, because this is the only chance you have to say no.'

Orla gulped. Her whole body resonated with his words, humming with anticipation, but some remnant of her defensive shield was still in place. Not yet smashed to pieces by this man. If she said yes to this... it was huge. The other night had been an aberration, a moment out of time. They'd been strangers. But this decision would be taken in all consciousness, knowing exactly who he was. She could barely contemplate the significance or the potential fallout. She shook her head even though it felt like the hardest thing in the world.

'No,' she whispered with little conviction, 'I don't want this.'

Antonio's face went even tighter. He was shutting down, closing off. Orla had a vision of seeing him tomorrow after the inevitable sleepless night she was about to endure. She could already feel the frustration clawing at her insides, her body rejecting her words.

And once again all other concerns were fading fast into the background.

Antonio was stepping back and already she felt even that distance like a gulf of gigantic proportions. He turned around and something in Orla rose up, something wild and visceral and feral. That rejection of her own words, so strong now that she couldn't ignore it. Still, he was almost at the door before she could let it out and it emerged like a raw cry. *'Stop!'*

# CHAPTER SIX

ANTONIO STOPPED AND relief was sweet and treacherous through Orla. But he didn't turn. She knew this moment was huge. She was throwing caution to the wind. Grabbing at pleasure. Stepping into danger, into the unknown. But the *necessary*. She needed this man like she needed to breathe, right now.

'Stop,' she said, stronger this time, firmer. 'I don't want you to go. Stay.'

Antonio turned and something clicked into place inside Orla. An assertion. That this was right.

He looked fierce and elemental in the soft lights which threw his face into sharp relief. Something quivered through her: recognition of a mate. But before that could freak her out, he uttered a guttural-sounding 'Come here.'

And without a conscious thought in her head, because it had been replaced with sheer blind instinct, Orla went to him.

It felt like they melted into each other. Her arms were around his neck; one of his hands was in her hair, cupping her head, the other across her back like a steel bar, welding her to his hard body.

It was a spontaneous combustion. They kissed and

it was desperately passionate. Mouths open, tongues duelling, as if they'd never get enough of kissing like this. Somewhere deep inside Orla something melted but she was too hot to think about it now.

Antonio drew back and said roughly, 'Bedroom.'

Orla sucked in deep breaths, slightly shocked at how fast her heart was beating already.

'The door on the left.'

As soon as the words left her lips she was being lifted up into Antonio's arms and he was carrying her through her living room to the bedroom. Just like the first time, a part of her thrilled at this display of cavemanlike masculinity in spite of her very feminist principles. Unable not to, Orla reached up to touch his jaw and felt the growth of stubble. Her body tightened with need.

He shouldered his way into the room where one lamp sent out a soft glow casting everything into shadow. He stopped by the bed and slowly, provocatively, slid Orla down the length of his body until she was standing in front of him.

Without taking her eyes off his, she kicked off her shoes, dropping a couple of inches in height. His hands went to the tiny buttons at the front of her dress and she could feel his frustration build when they proved too delicate for him.

She swatted his hands away. 'Let me.' Her own hands weren't much better though, shaking. She bit her lip and Antonio put out a hand, cupping her jaw, a thumb freeing her lower lip.

And then, interrupting her button undoing, he uttered something guttural in French and tipped up her head so that he could claim her mouth again as if he couldn't help himself. Orla's hands went to his arms to try and remain upright. She hadn't even undone all the buttons yet but the flames of desire were licking up around them and then her own hands were searching frantically for his shirt, undoing his buttons now.

His jacket had already disappeared and Orla revelled in smoothing her hands across his bare chest when his shirt fell open. Damp heat moistened between her legs and she could feel Antonio's hands go to her dress, pulling it up, one of his hands finding her panties and delving under the silk fabric. *Had she worn silk because all along she'd hoped this would happen?*—the insidious voice in her head resounded but Orla blocked it out.

His hand was cupping her butt cheek now, making her groan softly, pressing closer to Antonio, hips circling against him. When his hand explored deeper, fingers searching along the seam of her body, finding and releasing her wetness, she groaned in earnest.

Their mouths hadn't parted and now their breaths were suspended as Antonio's wicked fingers stroked Orla intimately. She broke away, looking up into that dark, dark gaze. Shocked all over again at how visceral this desire between them was.

'I need you. Now.'

Orla's body responded to his words as if she'd been set on fire from the inside out. Shirt hanging open, Antonio took his hands off her body to open his belt and undo his trousers, pushing them and his underwear to the floor in one movement.

Orla couldn't stop her gaze dropping and the anticipation in her body almost shot off the Richter scale when she saw him so aroused and ready. He'd been big before, but now he looked even bigger than she remembered.

He was bending, reaching under her dress for her underwear, tugging it down her hips and legs. Unsteady on her feet, Orla fell back onto the bed, and Antonio threw her panties to the side. With his big hands, he pushed up the dress until it pooled in a silken mass around her belly.

Orla knew she should be feeling wanton, or wicked or something. But she couldn't drum it up over the intense need. Antonio straightened up, tall. Proud. A warrior. Then he went and sat down in the armchair beside her bed. She came up awkwardly on her elbows to see him looking dark and brooding. He was ripping the foil off a condom and smoothing the rubber over his erection.

'Come here, Orla.'

Orla somehow managed to get up from the bed, her dress falling down over her legs, and gaping open at the front where she'd had to leave her buttons because it had proved too much of a challenge to undo them. She walked over to him and he reached for her, hands spanning her waist, pulling her onto him so that she had to straddle him, knees locked tight by his thighs and hips.

She gasped when he brought her down, her body rubbing against his arousal, caught between them. He brought up his hands and she thought he was going to attempt the buttons again but with a feral sound he put his hands to the delicate material and pulled it apart, making buttons pop and the silk rip.

To her shock, Orla found that instead of being angry, she felt excited by his impatience.

He looked at her. 'I'll buy you a new one.'

His hands were already busy at her back, undoing her bra so that it loosened and fell forward. Orla's arms were still slightly constrained by the dress which Antonio hadn't pulled off completely. It heightened the sensations building in her body, between her legs where she could feel him.

He pulled the lace cups of her bra down, making her breasts pop free, and cupped them with his hands, thumbs moving back and forth over the hard tips.

Orla's head went back and she squeezed her eyes shut against the delicious friction. Without even realising it she was already moving against him, up and down, seeking a deeper connection between their bodies. His erection slid tantalisingly close to where she wanted him to slip inside her and she could almost imagine his clenched jaw.

He shifted slightly so that the head of his penis rested at her entrance properly, no more teasing. Orla hovered now, suspended, her thigh muscles screaming with tension. She lifted her head up, eyes opening to look down at that harshly drawn dark face. Antonio had taken his hands off her breasts and put them on her waist, holding her still, poised over him, ready to sink down and take him into her.

Her body seemed to weep with desire, inner muscles already clenching with greedy anticipation. And then in the same moment as he brought her down onto his steel-hard arousal, he bent forward and put his mouth to one breast, encompassing the entirety of her aureole and nipple, and suckled her fiercely.

Orla's hands went to his head. She bit back a scream to feel him surging up into her body, so thick and hard. Filling her completely, more than her wildest fantasies since she'd been with him last.

His mouth on her breast, his body embedded in

hers…she could feel herself starting to splinter already but Antonio had other ideas. He took his mouth off her and looked into her eyes and slowly, masterfully, brought her up and back down, making the tremors recede a bit…but drawing out the torture.

Orla's hips wanted to move of their own volition, following the urges of her body, and there was an intense battle of wills between them. Both their faces flushed, breathing heavy. She put a hand to the high back of the chair behind Antonio's head, hanging on to anything she could.

She was rising and falling now, in perfect synchronicity with him. The glide of his body in and out of hers more exquisite than anything she'd ever known on this earth.

Antonio leant forward again and put that hot mouth to her other breast, teeth nipping gently at the hard tip, making Orla want to scream. Her movements got more desperate, frenzied, as she rode him hard. Her hand was in a white-knuckle grip on the back of the chair and then Antonio's head reared back, leaving her breast as he brought her down onto his shaft with such force that Orla could swear he touched her heart. He was so deep, so hard.

She couldn't see straight, couldn't think. Everything was tightening, spiralling, coiling inside her. She couldn't hold on any more. She was already having mini-orgasms around his length as he drove in and out, ruthlessly.

Orla was almost sobbing now. Antonio cupped her breast possessively, fingers trapping a nipple. Pinching.

'*Come* for me.'

A tear leaked from Orla's eye as she gasped and finally tipped over the edge into the dizzying, sweeping rush of pleasure and heat and oblivion. Her body convulsed around Antonio's as he still thrust up powerfully and rhythmically…finally surging into her clasping body one last time before shuddering his own release underneath her.

Orla was still in the aftermath. Dazed. Her body was still clenching rhythmically around Antonio's. Milking him. A part of her ached in that moment to know what it would feel like to have him spill inside her, anointing her with his seed. She resented the barrier. But she couldn't wrap her head around that rogue thought now. Her brain felt melted.

Finally, as if she'd been held suspended by some greater force, she collapsed forward, her head going between Antonio's neck and shoulder, breathing roughly against his hot damp skin. The smell of musk and heat and sex in the air.

His arms wrapped around her, holding her there, against him. Their bodies were still intimately joined and Orla, who would have shunned such intimacy with anyone else, burrowed even deeper into Antonio's embrace. She'd never felt so protected—as if it was just them and this room and this amazing feeling of satisfaction curling through her blood and bones.

At some point Orla felt Antonio move but was too lethargic to help, as he stood up and took her with him. She winced when their bodies were no longer joined and felt him put her down on the bed.

He was disrobing her, pulling her ruined dress down her arms, lifting her slightly so that he could pull it free and down completely. And her bra.

She opened slumberous eyes to see him looming

over her and felt pole-axed all over again when her body tingled with fresh awareness. She'd never known it could be like this.

Antonio came down beside her on the soft king-size bed, resting a hand on her belly which quivered. Then he moved that big hand up until it cupped her breast, rousing her again, making her eyes widen and her breath hitch.

When he bent his head to kiss her, she wound her arms around his neck and pressed herself along his length, moving sinuously against his fast-recovering erection. She wanted him again. As much if not more than she just had.

Antonio pulled his head back for a second and said roughly, 'What is it you do to me?'

She didn't know because she could ask him the same question. To drown out the voice of her conscience in her head, Orla furrowed her fingers into his hair, clasping his head. She answered far more lightly than she felt, 'No talking, Chatsfield.'

And she pulled his head back down and drowned everything out by focusing on this heady rush.

Hours later, Orla woke and found herself draped across Antonio's broad chest, arms wrapped around him. Mortified, she tried to extricate herself but to her surprise Antonio's arm, which was around her, tightened and he growled softly, 'Where do you think you're going?'

Orla's heart thumped, hard. 'Nowhere,' she whispered, and tried to relax again even though all she could think about was how it felt to have every inch of her body pressed to Antonio's. His hand started to move lazily up and down her back, fingers barely touching her skin, but setting off tiny explosions of sensations just the same.

She put her cheek back down on his chest and had to close her eyes for a second at the pang of emotion that coursed through her. The light outside the windows was changing ever so subtly. Not quite dawn but the end of the night had come. It made Orla feel absurdly as if they were cocooned from everything.

Something was shifting inside her and she couldn't stop it. Something very fundamental had changed during that dinner, and afterwards. As if she could deny it or tell herself it was just post-coital bliss, Orla broke the silence. 'You weren't sleeping?' she asked.

He must have shook his head because she felt a little movement and then he said, 'I haven't slept properly for years....'

Their voices were low, soft. Adding to this feeling of being out of the world slightly.

'The Legion?' Orla asked, just saying the two words.

Again she felt that movement that must have been Antonio nodding. Her body was heavy against his, heavy with a kind of satisfaction and peace she'd never known before.

Giving into curiosity, she asked him softly, 'What was it like?'

Antonio's hand stilled in its hypnotic motion up and down Orla's back. Her voice had been so low that she thought perhaps he hadn't heard...but she felt the tension in his body. She started to say, 'It's OK—'

But then he was talking and she closed her mouth again.

'It was the hardest thing I've ever done. But it was also intensely exciting and liberating.'

'Why was it liberating?' She felt him tense a little more.

He sighed. His chest moving beneath her cheek. 'Because for the first time in my life I wasn't a Chatsfield with all the accompanying acres of newsprint. The misconceptions, notoriety and expectations. I was…Marco Rossi.'

Orla lifted her head and rested her chin on her hand on his chest. But she couldn't see his face in the gloom. 'Rossi?'

'My mother's maiden name.'

Softly she said, 'It must have been hard to walk away and leave your family behind. Your sister.'

Antonio took a minute to answer, almost long enough for Orla to think he wouldn't. But then he said, 'It was. But she told me to go. She knew I needed to get away before I became suffocated.' His voice sounded bitter. 'And as my father had helpfully pointed out, I wasn't their father. *He* was.'

Orla's heart clenched. 'You and your sister shouldn't have had to take over…. You were so young.'

'We had no choice. We had a baby sister. We had to keep it together. Keep things running, stable. At least they were in schools most of the time and there was always money….'

Antonio couldn't believe that he was talking about this to Orla. But there was something different about the way she asked the question that almost every woman inevitably asked. *They* wanted to hear about the glamour and danger. And Antonio knew instinctively that Orla didn't. She asked to know about the real reality.

He felt the lightest of touches on one of the circular marks on his chest and he tensed, expecting her to ask about that...but she didn't. She asked, 'That tattoo on your arm...is it a coat of arms?'

Antonio relaxed again. 'It's the Legion's coat of arms.' He found himself smiling. 'I got it in a tattoo parlour in Marseilles on my first period of leave.... Don't ask me why. I was so drunk that night they could have tattooed a picture of Britney Spears on my arm and I wouldn't have noticed.'

He felt Orla huff a little chuckle. 'I think your street cred is still intact.'

Overcome with a sensation of losing his footing even though he was lying down, Antonio shifted them so that Orla was sprawled across his body, her breasts flattened against his chest.

He felt the hitch in her breathing; his hand became firmer on her back, sweeping up and down the silky skin, cupping her buttocks, squeezing gently and then harder. Telling her of his desire.

Needing no further encouragement, Orla's head dipped and her mouth met his in a sweet kiss. So sweet that it set something aching inside Antonio, in his chest. In a second though, digging his fingers into her hair, clasping her head, he'd changed it to something much more carnal.

And as Orla groaned her approval and her body started to move against his, seeking for more, Antonio blanked his mind and body of anything but this urgency. Driving away the questions as to what the hell had just passed between them...

* * *

The following day, Orla still felt raw after what had happened the previous evening…and night. Between her legs was tender, burning slightly but in a wickedly delicious way. That sense of something having shifted was still strong, too strong for her to deny.

It was taking her mind off work. Making her want to stand and dream about *him*. About the things he'd revealed to her. She was losing sight of who he was and why he was there in the first place and that made Orla exceedingly nervous. Perhaps he was playing her? Distracting her. Seducing her. So that she'd be left so weak and—

Just then there was a flurry of activity at the doors of the hotel and Orla's attention snapped back to the lobby. When she saw her mother appear from behind the reception desk to rush forward and greet what appeared to be an army of glamorous older ladies, Orla felt her chest sinking.

*Oh, Mother, please, not today*, she begged silently.

Antonio watched the interplay between Orla and her mother, who had apparently returned the day before ahead of her husband from where he was still wrapping up business in South-East Asia. It was clear where Orla got her looks from. The older woman was elegance personified, tall and slim with only the slightest hint of middle-aged spread. Her red hair fading slightly with age. But there the similarity ended. Orla's mother had a look of distinct petulance about her. Unaware of the guests milling around them, when he could see Orla was constantly aware, keeping an eye on everything.

Her face was strained. From where he was seated in the lobby he could hear snippets of their conversation.

'Mother, it's just not practical to bring twenty of your friends in for afternoon tea. You'll swamp the front reception area and you know how they get after a few drinks.'

Her mother pooh-poohed her. 'Nonsense, darling. It's Tilly's birthday and if your father was here he'd never say no to me. Anyway, it's too late because they're here now.'

Antonio's eyes narrowed on Orla. In an instant he read the dynamics of the Kennedy family. There was a veritable flock of expensively perfumed women thronging the lobby as they greeted one another and exclaimed loudly. It was the Ladies Who Lunch brigade and Orla's mother was the Queen Bee.

He could see Orla's frustration as they did exactly what she'd feared, taking over the serene peace of the main reception area off the lobby. She called one of the managers over and had a quiet word but his attempts to corral the ladies into a corner were unsuccessful once Mrs Kennedy had realised his instructions.

Antonio could see some of the other guests already getting up to leave, casting looks at the group. He knew that if he hadn't been staying here and hadn't seen Orla's work ethic, and he'd just witnessed this, he would have judged her passion for her brand as being shallow. It was anything but, especially if the pinched expression on her face was anything to go by.

She saw him then and her face went even paler. Two spots of colour blooming in her cheeks. He hadn't seen her since they'd woken at dawn that morning and made love again. While she'd been taking a shower, he'd left.

His head in a tangled mess after baring his soul in a way he hadn't done with another person apart from his therapist.

He lifted his hand and gestured for her to come to him and a predictably mutinous look came over her face, making his body tighten with awareness. Damn her and this ability she had to reduce him to the status of a horny teenager.

She walked towards him, her slim body graceful today in a cream silk shirt and slightly darker pencil skirt. Her hair immaculate, just begging for him to undo it and muss it up.

An image of a place popped into Antonio's mind's eye. And a desire to see Orla out of this milieu. Out of those too-structured clothes. A desire to see her naked and on her back, in his bed, for long hours at a time. Days, even. His heart sped up as an idea formed in his head and she sat down on the chair near him.

Immediately a staff member rushed over and asked if he could get them anything. Orla smiled and asked for tea. Antonio asked for coffee. He could hear the shrieks of laughter coming from Orla's mother's party now and saw her wince.

She caught his look and said, a little embarrassed, 'It wouldn't be so bad if I could persuade Mother to go to a private room but she won't hear of it. She likes to show off the hotel to her friends.'

Antonio tried not to let the fact that he could see how much this pained her affect him. He cursed himself; he shouldn't have slept with her. A voice in his head laughed uproariously at that. As if he'd had a choice.

And then he made a split-second decision. He told Orla that he'd be back in a few minutes and stood up, taking out his phone to make a call. Then he went straight over to where Orla's mother sat.

Orla watched Antonio and her breathing stopped when she saw him bend down to talk to her mother. Marianne Kennedy knew who he was because she'd met him before with Orla's father when the takeover was being discussed initially. So Orla could see her mother's less than friendly expression.

But then it was changing and becoming distinctly friendlier. To Orla's chagrin, she felt something dark settle into the pit of her belly. And then she almost gasped out loud—was she actually feeling jealous of her own mother?

She stood up as much in agitation at that revelation as for any other reason, just as Antonio also stood and headed back to Orla with an enigmatic expression on his face. But he walked right by her and went to the hotel entrance where Orla could see that a luxury coach was pulling up.

Then her mother came past her in a haze of expensive scent and she stopped momentarily to say, 'Orla, darling, that Mr Chatsfield has just offered us a champagne reception in his hotel for Tilly's birthday.'

Orla looked at her and her jaw dropped. Her mother sniffed. 'I mean, it's the least he can do, really, I think, in the circumstances.'

Orla was too stunned to say anything and could only watch as her mother led her merry band of acolytes out of the Kennedy hotel and onto a bus. As soon as they were gone, serene calm descended again.

Antonio returned and Orla found that she was sitting back down into the chair because her legs felt weak. Antonio sat down and proceeded to drink his coffee as if nothing had just happened. She stared at him as if he'd grown two heads. He raised a brow. 'What? Your mother was causing you stress so I removed it.'

Orla's mouth opened and closed. The overriding thing she was feeling was something very ambiguous. No one had ever, ever, done something like that for her before. She didn't quite know how to react and she was fairly sure she should be angry but quite for what reason she wasn't sure.

Antonio gestured. 'Drink your tea. It'll be getting cold.'

Orla shook her head slowly, some of the shock wearing off. 'I can't believe you just did that.'

'When is your father due back?'

Orla took a sip of tea to restore some sense of reality and frowned. 'Not till next week. Selling up in Bangkok has proved to be more complicated than he'd expected but he won't hear of me going out to help him.'

Antonio looked at her. 'Because you advised him against it, didn't you?'

Orla blanched before guilty colour seeped up from her neck. She saw Antonio's expression turn grim.

'What was it?' he asked now. 'Your mother fancied hotels in the Far East to impress her friends?'

Orla avoided his eye, feeling prickly after his very unexpected show of support. 'It's none of your business why we took those decisions.'

'But *we* didn't, did we? Your father was influenced by your mother. I spoke to her just now, Orla. She has nothing more on her mind than—'

She cut him off fiercely, all of her defensive hackles raised. 'My mother is *not* shallow.' She coloured hotly. 'Well, that is…not like you think. When we started out we had nothing. She helped my father build everything up but she came from a well-off background, so she was never entirely comfortable with having nothing. But she loves my father. And he adores her.'

Orla stopped, breathing harshly. She couldn't leave it there. She'd said too much now. She wasn't even aware of the hubbub of the lobby going on around them, only wanting to wipe that judgemental look off Antonio's face.

'My father knew that he'd taken her from a life of relative luxury, so as soon as we started making money, he insisted that she not work any more.'

Orla suddenly realised something and spoke aloud almost as much to herself as to Antonio. 'He was as much an architect of the woman she is today as she was. She got seduced by the wealth, the things she could buy. Her influence over him. But I know she's scared to death of what's going to happen, even though she'd never admit it. That's why she's behaving as if nothing is wrong.'

Antonio said softly, 'And you stepped into the breach to take her place. You want to save the hotels, don't you? Somehow?'

Orla glared at him for a long moment for unsettling her and making her reveal what she had, and then blurted out, 'Of course I do. This is our family legacy. My father worked so hard for this. It's killing me to think that it'll be lost. The fact that our name will live on is small comfort when we know they won't really be our hotels.'

Orla's mouth tightened at her outburst. She blamed Antonio for making love to her so thoroughly that she felt raw and exposed, unable to protect herself. And for making her realise something about her mother that she'd never even really articulated to herself before.

'And yet, that's enough for your father,' Antonio surmised grimly. 'Have you talked to him about ways to save the business apart from just saving the brand name?'

Orla fought to control her wayward emotions, took another sip of lukewarm tea and put the cup down, as if this conversation wasn't costing her as much as it was.

She nodded slowly and admitted reluctantly, 'He doesn't want to know. He thinks that if we can save the name across as many hotels as possible, then he won't have failed completely. But I know we have a chance if he'll just agree to sell everything, name and all, apart from this flagship hotel and the ones in Dublin and New York.'

Antonio whistled softly. 'That's ambitious.'

Orla lifted her chin. 'We could do it though, if my father would just agree to talk about a much smaller investment with a partner, and to let all our other interests go, name and all. But he's stubborn. He either wants to retain as many of our hotels as he can, or none....'

Orla looked away from Antonio's narrowed gaze. To admit to this defeat, in front of him...was galling. Especially after last night, when she still felt wobbly and oversensitised and all over the place emotionally. Between her legs stung with the after-effects of his powerful body surging into hers over and over again.

She glanced back at him, suddenly acutely aware of how much she'd revealed. 'What are you doing, Antonio? You're hardly our ally. You don't care what happens to us as long as you get your precious deal to keep your sister happy.'

His face got darker at that and then he said gruffly, 'I've never pretended anything else is the case. But you can't deny that things have changed…between us.'

Orla's breath got choppy. 'No, I can't. But we should never have got involved—it's not a good idea.'

Antonio looked even darker. 'It was inevitable. If it hadn't happened that night, Orla, it would have happened after we'd met. That's just maths.'

Orla's chest felt tight. He leant forward then and she had to stop herself from moving back, afraid of the way her body responded so violently.

'I have a proposition for you.'

Orla's heart stopped and started again. Surely…he wasn't going to offer—

'Come away with me.'

# CHAPTER SEVEN

ORLA BLINKED AT HIM. For a crazy bizarre moment she'd thought that he might be about to offer to be the investor that they would need if she was to push her plan with her father. Wishful thinking. Of course he wasn't. He was as bound by blood as she was to get the outcome he wanted. She was nothing to him. And then his words sank in, belatedly.

She frowned. 'Come away with you…where?'

His eyes captivated her, making the hubbub of the lobby of the hotel fade away.

'I have a place in the south of France, near Saint-Raphaël. I bought it while I was in the Legion for my periods of leave.'

Orla's heart sped up; her belly grew tight. 'But… why?'

'Because I want you and you want me, and maybe if we have a few days together, on our own, this desire will burn out.'

Something about his coolly delivered reasoning and the fact that he wanted *this desire* to burn out made her recoil and want to protect herself. She stood up and said frostily, 'Thanks but no thanks. I have a job to do. In case it's escaped your notice we're in the middle of a takeover bid. Last night was a mistake and shouldn't be repeated.'

She was about to stalk away when Antonio caught her hand in a powerful grip and she looked down at him reluctantly, mindful of being under the scrutiny of staff and guests. His eyes compelled her though.

His voice was low but she heard the steel in it. 'The fact is that we can't be within ten feet of each other and not want each other. And to deny that is to deny a fact of life.'

Orla stared at him for a long moment, caught. She was losing her footing, feeling increasingly out of her depth.

With effort, she pulled her hand free and it tingled. Along with other parts of her body. She finally walked away from Antonio and that black gaze before he could see how turbulent her emotions were.

As she passed the reception area though, a waiter crossed her path with a tray full of the detritus of the empty glasses from Orla's mother's table. They'd already managed to open a few bottles of champagne before they'd been offered a better deal via Antonio. She stopped in her tracks.

Orla felt very vulnerable to recall that feeling of how Antonio had taken charge of a situation. For her. *Your mother was causing you stress so I removed it.* She hated to admit it, but a part of her thrilled to know that he had done that, even if it had been heavy-handed. She'd been proving herself for so long that she'd never had support herself.

Something sharp gripped her. Along the way Orla had sacrificed almost any personal desires. Relationships had been relegated to the periphery. She'd worked her fingers to the bone. Any holiday had been taken in one of their hotels with work as the main focus. She'd even missed out on girlfriends, as one by one they'd stopped calling because she was simply too busy.

Something rose up within her, anger and a sense of futility. She turned around and saw Antonio standing just feet away, watching her with that heavy-lidded gaze. Her insides clenched, hard.

*The fact is that we can't be within ten feet of each other and not want each other. And to deny that is to deny a fact of life.*

Just looking at him right now made her want him. He was right. He was also an assault on her senses and, more disturbingly, on her emotions and the walls she'd built around herself to concentrate on work for all these years. He made her forget that. He made her want more…like the home she'd always dreamed of.

But despite the vulnerability he precipitated within her, the thought of leaving this all behind—rebelling in a minute way for the first time in her life, doing something just for her—was so heady she nearly swayed. Running away with the enemy; you couldn't get more rebellious than that.

If he was going to stand over the smouldering wreck of their business, shouldn't she take what she could, while she could?

She forced her feet to move and she walked back over to Antonio, some intoxicating sense of feminine confidence filling her to see his eyes glitter, his gaze so intent on her, as if he'd just been waiting for her to admit she wanted this too. He wanted her. And she wanted him. He was right; it was that simple.

She would protect herself from those nebulous disturbing thoughts of a home and another life. They weren't real. This was.

She stopped in front of him and looked up and said with a huskiness that was the only indicator of her deep conflicting emotions, 'I've changed my mind. How soon can we leave?'

His eyes flashed and colour scored along those amazing cheekbones. He smiled and it was dark and wicked. It held no triumph though; if it had, Orla might have come to her senses.

'How soon can you pack?'

Orla was being whisked to a private airfield before the rashness of her actions and reality began to sink in, when the adrenalin that had fuelled her decision and the past hectic few hours was beginning to drain away.

As soon as she'd made the decision Antonio had allowed for no room to doubt it. He'd personally overseen her handing over the reins of control to her most senior manager. He'd then accompanied her up to her suite of rooms and had kissed her soundly, as if wanting to make sure she didn't forget why they were doing this.

He'd checked out of the hotel and was going to join her at the airfield after he'd paid a visit to the Chatsfield Hotel, presumably to tie up his own loose ends and reassure his sister that everything was on track and that taking their adversary on a debauched holiday was all part of the plan. If he was even admitting that he was doing such a thing.

Orla recalled the frisson of wicked danger she'd felt as she'd tidied up after the night before and hurriedly packed some essentials. Eschewing her structured work

clothes for the more casual ones she almost never got
to wear, because she invariably worked weekends. Pathetic.

Now, as London sped by outside the car that Antonio had sent for her, she couldn't help the burn of excitement from growing in her gut. She was doing the
rashest thing she'd ever done in her life. She winced
minutely—apart perhaps from that one-night stand.

Their solicitor had just looked at her. 'You're doing
what?'

Orla had striven to sound as cool and confident as
she could. 'I'm going away for a few days, Tom. Mr
Chatsfield has seen everything he needs to for now.
And I need a little time to think about our strategy.'

Her face had coloured then to imagine that that anal-
ysis of strategy would be taking place on her back in
Antonio's bed somewhere in France.

'Well, this is most unorthodox, Orla. What am I to
say to your father?'

Orla couldn't help a little sadness tingeing her voice.
'Tell him that everything is in hand, exactly how he
wants it.'

Because ultimately her father was never going to
compromise on his vision of how he wanted things to
be, and Antonio and the Chatsfields would get their
hands on the Kennedy Group in the end.

But right now Orla only felt a very fledgling sense
of…relief, of a weight being lifted off her shoulders,
which stunned her. When for so long her whole identity
had been bound up in her family business.

For the first time in her life she was deviating from
her strict code of conduct and she wasn't going to question it or doubt it, because waiting for her right now,

standing by a small private jet, was the tall figure of Antonio Chatsfield and Orla's mind blanked of anything but *him*.

Antonio watched the car approach and could see the petite shape of Orla in the back. His pulse grew fast, blood heating up. His jeans already felt tight against his crotch as he responded helplessly to even that provocation.

He'd told her earlier that he wanted her to come away with him so this desire could burn itself out, and she'd reacted with predictable spikiness. After all, he'd hardly couched it as a romantic proposition. But the truth was that his motivations for asking her to this place were far more complex.

He'd never asked anyone else here. His own family didn't even know he owned it. It was completely private, where he'd gone to battle the demons of his mind after the Legion and where he'd finally got well again. Or at least on the path to wellness.

But now he was bringing this woman and he could drum up no sense of regret. Only intense need. He wasn't afraid that Orla would get the wrong idea; he'd never met a more driven woman whose career came first. Well, apart from his own sister. His conscience struck him—he'd been deliberately vague with Lucilla about what he was doing, when he'd fired off an email telling her that he had to take care of some personal business. Which was true. She just didn't know how personal.

He frowned now as Orla's car pulled up and came to a halt. In fact, now that he thought of it, his sister's response had seemed distracted. Less than interested about his progress with the Kennedy Group, when it had been uppermost of her concerns just days ago. And had she in fact mentioned something about going away herself? He'd been so intent on avoiding her scrutinising his actions that he'd almost forgotten about that now....

But then the car door was opening and Antonio's mind emptied of anything else, except *this*. The sense of triumph that had gone through him when Orla had stopped and turned back to him in the hotel had been so strong that he'd had to hide it from her, knowing it would make her turn on her heel again.

As he went to open her door and saw her bright head of hair, down around her shoulders, and that beautiful face, triumph was only a fraction of what he was feeling. And what he was feeling was far too disturbing to focus on now. It made him think of how vulnerable she'd looked as she'd admitted to him how badly she wanted to save her hotels. And the reality behind her mother's brittle fun-loving facade.

Her defence of her mother had echoed within him, making him wonder about the reality behind the scandalous headlines of his own siblings. Bringing up that sense of fear at how his brothers and sister would react if he got in touch.

But now Orla's hand was slipping into his, scattering his thoughts, and he closed his fingers around hers and pulled her from the car, mindful of her delicacy in spite of the steely strength she hid it with. He took in the tight figure-hugging jeans and plimsolls. The pretty violet-coloured silk sleeveless top with a frilled neckline.

'Why, Ms Kennedy,' he drawled, 'I would have thought you were allergic to jeans.'

She scowled and pulled her hand free but her eyes were bright. Bright enough to mesmerise him.

'One more crack like that, Chatsfield, and you'll have to entertain yourself in your little hideaway.'

Antonio took her hand again and found himself feeling serious as he said, 'Not a chance. You're not escaping now.'

He pulled her towards the plane where some officials were waiting to check their passports and then he was allowing her to precede him up the steps and forcing his hands away from that pert backside. There would be time for that...later. All the time in the world. And then this hunger would have left his system and he could get on with his life.

'Wow.' Orla could only emit one ineffectual word as she stepped out of Antonio's Jeep when she saw the property laid out before her, about three hours later. It was stupendously idyllic.

The property was at the end of a long drive, set into a forest of gnarly trees with the glittering sea close enough to touch. Insects buzzed in the warm sultry air; Orla could taste the sea on her tongue.

The house itself made something very private within her resonate. That desire for *home*. It was a palatial villa. Three-storeyed. Lots of windows and huge central front doors with stone steps leading down to a charmingly haphazard pathway. The stones of the house were obviously well worn with age and the sun, cream in colour, and the roof was made up of terracotta slates. Quintessentially French.

Antonio's voice was gruff as he took Orla's hand. 'Come on, I'll show you around.'

Orla was afraid to look at him. Afraid he might see something she wasn't ready to reveal. The magnitude of what she was doing had hit her on the plane, some twenty thousand feet in the air, and instead of hurtling her back into reality it had only intensified her sense of excitement and rebellion and made her want this more.

The small plane had made Orla acutely aware of how gorgeous Antonio was in faded jeans and a polo shirt that stretched across his wide chest and powerful biceps. It had taken every last ounce of control not to jump on him there and then. But his knowing heavy-lidded looks had stopped her. She'd been loath to reveal how hot he made her feel, and so she'd sat on her hands and ignored his provocative glances as much as possible.

But now, with her hand in his…transported to another world, literally, everything felt much closer to the surface, stripped away. And Orla could feel her defences slipping and crumbling, much as they had when she'd allowed him into her rooms last night….

Antonio was leading her in through the main doors which were open, revealing a huge open-plan downstairs-reception area off which were several rooms. The walls were the original exposed bricks, and there were flagstone floors. Orla stifled a gasp when Antonio led her into a stunning formal dining room with open French doors that led out to a glorious side garden. It was exquisitely decorated in cooling tones of whites and greys.

A vase of extravagant colourful blooms was a centrepiece on a small serving table near the doors.

She heard Antonio remark dryly, 'Not bad for a meathead ex-soldier, hmm?'

Orla blushed. He was no meathead ex-soldier. She tried to cover her discomfiture and the realisation that this was not far off how she would have decorated such a space herself. She shrugged one shoulder lightly. 'Not bad, I guess.... The exposed walls add the requisite roughness.'

Antonio's eyes flashed dangerously but he just shook his head wryly before leading her on, into a very comfortable and homely den area with state-of-the-art TV and music systems. Bookshelves lined the walls and were bursting with books. To diguise the growing sense of vulnerability to see yet another piece of her innermost desires manifesting, Orla quipped, 'I presume the books are just for show?'

'Cheeky.' His hand tightened on hers and she was about to look up when a high-pitched shriek pierced the air and seemingly out of nowhere a tiny blur of brown limbs and black hair ran through the other side of the den, quickly followed by a similar smaller blur, also shrieking.

For a second Orla was just in shock and confusion... until she registered the way her entire body had pulsated with what felt like a wave of longing. It was so strong that she didn't even realise how tightly she was gripping Antonio's hand until he squeezed back and said, 'Hey, it's only Marie-Ange's kids.'

Orla stared at him blankly. It took seconds for his words to sink in—to realise that what she'd just seen hadn't been some projection of her deepest fantasies. That she wasn't going totally mad. Then she recalled the open front door...

A lyrical sing-song voice called out, and then a young, dark-haired attractive woman appeared, taking off an apron as she walked in. Antonio let Orla's hand go to greet the woman warmly, kissing her on both cheeks.

She smiled prettily, showing dimples, and Orla could only watch as Antonio turned back to her to say, 'I'd like you to meet Marie-Ange, my housekeeper. She and her husband, Dominic, look after the place for me while I'm not here. They live in the local village.'

The woman was smiling so widely that Orla couldn't help but respond, despite the shock she'd received. They shook hands, and just then the two children exploded into the room again and Antonio caught one up and held him high, where he squealed with delight.

The woman was explaining in charmingly accented English, 'Please excuse the disturbance—I was hoping to be long gone by now but Dominic had a crisis with his car this morning and we had to go to the garage and then he had to take my car…and I had to take the kids….' She smiled with that long-suffering look of the slightly harassed mum.

Orla had seen it countless times in the hotel and had always done her best to make sure both mother and children were accommodated.

She smiled and muttered something vague, acutely aware of Antonio with the small boy in his arms, speaking to him in French. The other child, a little girl, a toddler, equally cute, was clinging on to Antonio's leg, her huge brown eyes imploring him to lift her up. Seeing Antonio so at ease with these children made something quiver inside her.

But then Marie-Ange was lifting her daughter away from Antonio's leg and instructing her children firmly to leave Mr Chatsfield and his guest alone. She was speaking in a flurry of fast French to Antonio, who had put the little boy down. He responded with a very Gallic expression that was a universal sign for *don't worry*. Orla's French was passable but not fluent.

Antonio kissed Marie-Ange again, and Orla reeled a little to see this side of him and to see the obvious warmth he felt for this woman. The little girl was in Marie-Ange's arms, a thumb in her mouth, eyes disconcertingly steady on Orla.

Orla had never really contemplated the reality of having children. When would she have the time? But when she'd seen these two jump out of nowhere and streak through the room like little ghosts—that feeling of longing had been so intense, she still shook with it. It was as if her biological clock had just started with a resounding bang.

Marie-Ange was leaving, calling goodbye, her son rushing ahead of her. And then they were gone. Antonio turned to Orla, something enigmatic in his eyes. He arched a brow. 'You got a shock to see Marie-Ange and the kids? I should have told you….'

Terrified that he might guess at the seismic revelation seeing those children had precipitated within her, Orla just shrugged minutely. 'I was startled, that's all. I hadn't expected anyone else to be here.' It was only now that she recalled seeing another car near the entrance of the property, back up the drive.

Something else came into Antonio's expression then, something far more recognisable. Desire. And Orla welcomed it—anything to avoid thinking about what had just happened.

Throatily Antonio said, 'We won't be disturbed again unless we want to be.'

He took her hand again and started tugging her in the direction of the stairs which led to the upper levels from the reception area. 'I'll show you the rest of downstairs later. Right now I'm more interested in showing you where we'll be sleeping.'

Desire, wicked and hot, burst into Orla's solar plexus. Relieved again to be moving away from far too disturbing and scary revelations, she said nothing as Antonio led her up to a second level and down the flagstoned hallway covered with rugs to an open door.

A majestic bedroom was revealed, spanning the width of the house, with breathtaking views out over the rest of the property and the sea and the gathering dusk. A soft neutral-coloured sisal-type carpet covered the floor. White drapes billowed gently in the fragrant warm breeze.

But all Orla could see was the enormous superking-size bed in the centre of the room, covered in white linen. Antonio let her hand go and came to stand in front of her. Orla gazed at him and gulped.... He looked so feral. Dangerous.

Surprising her, he cupped her jaw gently. 'Thank you, for coming here with me.'

Something tender gripped her inside. What was it about this man that kept her so thrown? So unsure of what he was about to do next?

Wanting to diffuse the emotions, Orla said provocatively, 'I haven't *come*...yet.'

A ghost of a smile made one side of Antonio's mouth quirk and to Orla's endless relief he pulled her into him. Roughly he said, 'I think I can remedy that within a short matter of time....'

And then his mouth was covering hers and lust was rising and pushing down all the scary things that Antonio made her think of and feel. This she could handle....

The other? Not so much. Orla made a vow to herself before Antonio's wicked mouth and hands rendered her completely senseless to avoid straying off this lust-fuelled path as much as possible while they were here.

And she also said a silent prayer, as he deposited her on the soft surface of the bed, that this desire *would* blaze out between them and leave her free to resume her life. Free of far too disturbing wants and desires that had never really risen to bother her before.

The dawn light bathed Orla's pale, pale skin in a pinky glow. She was on her front, arm curled close to her chest where Antonio could see the fleshy curve of her breast, one leg straight, one leg bent. Her bare backside was surprisingly plump for someone so slim and petite. The sheet had long ago fallen from the bed. In fact, Antonio thought wryly as he rested his head on one hand and regarded her, he was surprised all the sheets hadn't burned off the bed altogether.

His smile faded as he went back to his slow perusal of his lover. *His lover.* He'd never had a lover like Orla before. Her face was towards him, resting on one cheek. Lashes long and dark against her skin, mouth pouting softly, swollen from his kisses. Her hair a vibrant splash of red on the white linen. Needless to say, even just looking at her like this had his body in a painful state of arousal. After making love to her endlessly, all night. Until exhaustion had finally claimed them.

He had never allowed a woman to spend more than a night or two at the most in his bed. That had been as much a conditioning of his career as anything else. But even before he'd embarked on life in the Legion, he'd avoided anything but the most fleeting intimacy like the plague.

He could remember a time when his parents' marriage had been relatively happy. Solid. But he could also remember how quickly it had fallen apart. As if it had never been held together by much except superficialities in the first place. Antonio had long suspected his father of his infidelities before it had become fact. Even before his wife had crumbled completely and left.

He thought of Orla's muted reaction to seeing Marie-Ange's children the previous day and recalled how he'd felt a bizarre sense of regret. What was that all about? He knew how much Orla had invested in her career; she was the kind of woman who might never marry. He certainly couldn't see her in an apron baking cookies for happy chocolate-covered children…and yet…the image slid into his mind with shocking ease, mocking him. He could see it all too clearly. And the fact that he could even drum up such an image made him break out in a cold sweat.

Antonio's mouth firmed as he caught his line of thinking and the direction it was taking. It had been a long time since he'd ruminated on such things as his parents' failed marriage and he had *never* speculated about a lover and whether or not they wanted children. So why on earth was he thinking of this now when he'd resigned himself to the fact long ago that he had no intention of walking down that path himself? Just because a woman lay in his bed?

*Not just any woman*, spoke a rogue voice in his ear.

Antonio made a silent sound of rejection at that and instead of doing what he really wanted to do, which was to wake Orla and tumble them both over the edge again, he forced himself to get out of the bed and told himself a six-mile run would empty his mind of such unwelcome imaginings. And hopefully put a dent in his insatiable libido.

As Orla woke slowly through mists of consciousness, she became aware of the slight aches and muscle pains in her body. *Antonio.* Her eyes flew open and she squinted in the light of the early-morning sun streaming in the open window.

But she knew that the bed was empty beside her. She breathed out and then in. The tantalising scent of fresh-growing lavender tickled her nostrils.

As much as the bereft feeling registered, she also felt a tiny bit relieved. She couldn't think straight when Antonio was near her. He seemed to short-circuit her brain.

She realised she was stark naked, and that the covers had long disappeared, but instead of reaching to find a cover, Orla let the feeling of half-uncomfortable wickedness wash over her. She felt wanton. And thoroughly satisfied. And in the morning light, all of the disturbing notions Marie-Ange's children had precipitated felt very distant and silly.

Orla heard a rattle of noise downstairs and her body tightened even at that. She got up and saw that her bag and his had been brought in from the Jeep. She blushed to think of how they'd gone straight to bed and hadn't even left it to eat or wash.

She took out some toiletries and found the huge en-suite bathroom with its wet-room shower. In an instant she was rewarded with a lurid fantasy of what it would be like to have Antonio lift her against the wall so that he could pound into her body while water ran over their bodies.

Cursing her rampant X-rated imagination, Orla quickly washed and dried herself off. She put on a pair of shorts and a sleeveless T-shirt and felt like a teenager all over again. It had been a long time since she'd worn such casual clothes and it tugged at something vulnerable inside her. Like when Antonio had mocked her gently for wearing jeans. Or how she'd felt when she'd admitted she'd been a tomboy.

Halting at the top of the stairs leading down, Orla had to put a hand to her chest for a second. Her heart was beating so rapidly. She had a sudden sense of just how dangerous this man was to her. How easily he was seeing into a part of her she'd not revealed to anyone. Fear gripped her. She vowed in that moment that when she saw him she'd tell him that she couldn't afford more than a couple of days at the most in this place.

A couple of days... Surely she could keep herself immune from him in that time, and emerge intact?

Biting her lip, Orla made her way downstairs, dreading seeing Antonio because she knew she'd forget everything again and start drowning. But when she walked barefoot into the kitchen, her vow to herself of *just a couple of days* flew out the window and, as she'd feared, she drowned.

She was faced with the mouthwatering sight of Antonio's bare back, tapering down to lean hips upon which a pair of battered cargo shorts hung precariously. A towel was slung around his neck and his hair was wet. He whistled softly as something that smelled delicious sizzled on a pan on the stove.

The only thing marring the idyllic picture were the

copious scars that criss-crossed Antonio's back. Some faint and silvery, others uglier raised welts of skin. Orla's chest tightened and she must have emitted some kind of a sound because he turned around and his gaze swept her up and down so hungrily that she blushed, feeling shy. Which was ridiculous.

'Hey, you looked so peaceful this morning I didn't want to wake you.'

Orla came forward and something leapt inside her when Antonio reached for her and pulled her into his side. He was hot.

She looked up. 'How long have you been up?'

He glanced down and winked at her salaciously and said, 'I'm always up for you, honey.'

Orla mock-hit him and squirmed out from under his arm and stood back. This teasing Antonio was far too...seductive and disturbing to her equilibrium. Also, it hinted at that slightly rougher side of him. A side that was less in evidence now as she'd got to know him. Wanting to cover up her self-consciousness Orla glanced at the pan and said, 'I didn't know you could cook.'

Antonio diverted his attention back to the delicious-looking eggs and onions and mushrooms. 'We all had to take turns cooking in the army and while it was nothing spectacular, barely edible, when I left I discovered that I wanted to learn how to do it properly.'

His face had tightened up, a tension appearing in his shoulders. But Orla didn't push it. He was serving the food up now on two plates and instructing her to get the pot where fresh coffee had been percolating.

Orla repressed a smile at his inherently bossy tone.

She'd been so naive when she'd accused him of being bossy the first night they'd met.

When Orla took her first mouthful of scrambled eggs and mushrooms and onions and garlic, she swallowed and said with not a little surprise, 'This is *good*.'

Antonio shrugged modestly and quipped, 'It'd be a bit of a disaster if I couldn't manage something as basic as this.'

Orla coloured and bent her head over the plate but Antonio must have seen it and he said, 'Don't you cook?'

Orla speared some food and shook her head quickly. 'Never had the opportunity.' She chewed and swallowed. 'I told you that we always lived at the hotel.... I wasn't used to home cooking.'

Antonio had hoovered up his food and sat back now, cup of coffee in his hand, supremely relaxed. Supremely gorgeous.

'So...' he said lazily, 'this house of yours, the one you always wanted. Do you know where it is?'

Orla couldn't get any hotter. She took a quick sip of coffee herself as if that might help. But Antonio was just watching her, and waiting. Feeling something subside inside her, Orla gave in. 'I do actually. It's in Notting Hill.'

Antonio arched a brow.

Orla felt like squirming but she went on. 'Sometimes, on my days off—'

'You have days off?' came Antonio's mock-incredulous tone.

Orla stuck her tongue out at him and started again. 'As I was saying, sometimes on my days off I'll look up properties for sale and request a viewing. I know it's not really fair to make the agents think I'm an interested buyer....' She shrugged, feeling stupid now.

Antonio's voice was slightly husky. 'And what do you do?'

Orla glanced at him suspiciously in case he was laughing at her but the serious expression in his eyes almost made her feel more self-conscious. Reluctantly she revealed, 'I go and look around, mentally decorating the house, figuring out what rooms I'd use for what. Where my furniture would go.'

Desperate to get Antonio's focus off her, Orla asked quickly, 'What about you? Don't you want to return to your house?'

Antonio practically shuddered and went tight-lipped. 'No. I left that house a long time ago. My brother Nicolo, the one who was injured in a fire, he lives there now, and he's welcome to it.'

'And what about your brothers and sisters? Are you going to see them?'

Antonio stared at Orla and he wondered how it was that she was able to slice right into him with her soft questions, more accurately than a blade seeking a vital artery. And then he thought of how she'd squirmed to admit to looking at houses in her spare time. He still felt tight inside to think of her walking around those empty houses, dreaming.

'The truth is,' admitted Antonio, 'I've been in touch with all of them periodically over the years. I just haven't actually seen any of them, apart from Lucilla and Cara. And Orsino when he was in Afghanistan to do some crazy extreme skydive.'

'You shouldn't feel guilty for leaving them.'

'I don't,' Antonio snapped back, so fast that he saw Orla flinch slightly.

Immediately remorse filled him and he cursed softly. 'I'm sorry…. I just… Well, maybe I do feel guilty.'

'Your father is still alive,' Orla pointed out. 'He should have been there and he had no right to turn around and lambaste you just because you were doing his job for him.'

Antonio smiled at the touch of defiance in her tone. He'd like to see her meet his father one day; his arrogant old man wouldn't know what'd hit him. Realising how incendiary that thought was, projecting Orla into a future situation, Antonio stood up and cleared the plates.

He said over his shoulder, 'I cooked, so you can wash the plates.'

He heard Orla's chair against the flagstoned floor and then a cheeky, 'Aye-aye, sir.'

He looked behind him to see her standing to attention, hand angled at her forehead in a salute, and had to bite the inside of his cheek to repress a smile. When the urge had passed he said with lethal softness, 'Are you looking for punishment for being so cheeky?'

Orla blushed prettily and came over to the sink. She fluttered her eyelashes at him. 'Yes, please. Sir.'

He took her chin between his thumb and forefinger and had to stop himself from plundering that soft mouth. He could control this rampant desire. He *could*.

'Very well then, Private Kennedy. It'll be a three-mile swim in the ocean as soon as you've finished washing up.'

Already he could feel her breath quickening against his hand which wasn't helping his resolve.

'Very well, sir. I'll get this out of the way and get my bikini—'

Antonio shook his head, cutting her off, and smiled wolfishly. 'No bikini required, Private Kennedy. You'll be swimming naked.'

# CHAPTER EIGHT

ORLA FELT THE SWEAT dripping into her eyes and wiped it away. Her chest hurt with her laboured breathing and her heart was like a piston in her chest. It was all she could do to keep her eyes on the feet and legs in front of her and follow their steps.

When she could spare more than a breath she said, 'Has anyone ever told you you're a sadist?'

A faintly humorous-sounding 'Too many times to recall' came back to her on the warm breeze. And then a hand came into her vision and Orla grabbed it with the both of hers and let Antonio pull her up beside him at the summit of the hill.

The stunning view made the pain in her legs and pounding heart dissipate as she sucked in oxygen. Orla wiped more sweat from her brow with the back of her hand. She felt unbearably hot and sticky even though she was wearing shorts and a singlet vest. She wasn't even wearing the pack of supplies, as Antonio was. And her legs felt rubbery. But she also felt exhilarated as she looked out over a breathtaking view of the Côte d'Azur and the glittering sea beyond.

Antonio's villa lay nestled in the trees far, far below

them. His swimming pool was just visible in a flash of blue, making her long to dive in.

'Here, you should drink lots of water.'

Orla accepted the bottle eagerly and drank deeply. When she handed it back she scowled to see him barely out of breath or glowing with sweat.

She grumbled, 'Just because you're used to running twenty miles with a pack of stones on your back…'

He smiled as he said, 'More like thirty miles with fifteen-to twenty-kilogram weight backpacks.'

Orla's eyes widened. 'That's suicidal.'

Antonio's face got shuttered and he turned away from her. He shrugged minutely. 'It's one way of determining who has got what it takes.'

Orla looked at his remote profile for a long moment before pushing down the questions that bubbled up. Antonio always clammed up when she asked him anything about his time in the Legion. As if he was too close to the source in some way.

It had been three days since that morning in the kitchen followed by the very erotic naked swim in the sea. Orla could have laughed at the vow she'd made to stay for two days and then leave.

As she'd feared, she'd been sucked into a bubble of sensuality. And, more disturbingly, a kind of freedom she'd never experienced before: waking up late, making love, eating, swimming naked in the sea…wearing as little as possible in general. Eating again, making love, sleeping.

In some respects, Orla felt as if she were nine years old again…that tomboy girl, always eager to run free and get into scrapes. Living on the edge. Before everything had changed. Before she'd sacrificed her deepest desires and forgotten what she really wanted.

She must have shivered or something because Antonio said gruffly, 'I told you to wear a hat.'

He was taking his pack off and bending down to open it, presumably to search for her hat which she'd made a face at earlier. Now he took it out and looked stern, plonking it on her head, over where her hair was piled high in a messy bun.

'And *don't* take it off. You'll get sunstroke.'

He took out cream and Orla saw him pour some into his hands. 'Turn around,' he instructed bossily, and his big hands made short work of smoothing the suncream into her bare shoulders, neck and arms. And despite the heat, she could feel the effect on her body and lamented the fact that this *desire* was showing no signs of waning.

When he squatted down in front of her to do her legs, Orla put up a pathetic protest but Antonio was already slathering cream right up under the hem of her shorts, fingers coming far too close to where her body was swelling, ripening for his touch.

His fingers swept close to the V of her legs and she smacked his hands away, saying breathlessly, 'I really will get sunstroke if you keep that up and we make love up here on the mountaintop.'

Antonio smiled devilishly and replied, 'Damn the sun anyway, and your delicate Irish complexion.'

He stood up and took up the backpack again and said, 'There's a shaded spot to have some lunch nearby. Let's keep going.'

The thought of shade and the possibility… Orla's inner muscles spasmed with lust but she just said lightly, 'Aye-aye, sir.'

As he walked on and she followed, she had to bite her lip against the lightness building inside her. These moments of spreading joy at being in this man's company—and his bed—were becoming far too frequent and disturbing.

Marie-Ange and her husband had called by the previous day with their children. She and Marie-Ange had played with the children together in the sea while Antonio and Dominic had barbecued dinner. Then they'd sat around the pool in the gathering dusk, Dominic's daughter, Lily, asleep on his lap and Pierre, their son, asleep on Antonio's. That hitherto dormant longing for children had surged up within Orla again.

She had to face it: something was changing within her. Her life and career, the hotel, all felt very far away. She felt as if she wouldn't fit back into that world as neatly again, as if some edges had been rubbed off her.

Antonio was leading her into a shaded clearing with rocks that served neatly as chairs and a table. Orla sat down and took off the hat, fanning herself with it gratefully. He took out some bread, ham and cheese, a chilled bottle of water, and one of sparkling wine. Something incredibly tender washed through her.

Antonio handed her a crude sandwich of ham and cheese and she took it, her mouth already watering. He came and sat on the rock beside her, long legs stretched out, and they ate in companionable silence, sipping the water and wine.

At one point he said a touch ruefully, 'It's not exactly what you're used to.'

Orla ducked her face down, pretending an absorption in a speck of dirt on her leg. 'It's fine.' She would have chosen this crude picnic over any number of fancy

dinners in fancy restaurants anywhere else in the world.
And that realisation told her once and for all, resound-
ingly, that she would never end up like her mother. Seduced by the glitter of new wealth. Something like relief
flowed through her, as if it had been a subliminal fear
for years.

'I notice that you're not coming out in a rash not to
be wearing one of your smart dresses or suits.'

Something unwelcome lanced Orla, a reminder of
reality. And she pushed it down, deep. She scowled at
Antonio, who was looking far too innocent. And gorgeous. His tan had deepened even more in the sun, making him look even more darkly sexy.

He reached out a hand and his thumb touched her
lower lip, tugging it gently. His eyes were on her mouth
and then lifted to hers. They'd gone dark, smoky. 'I
think I prefer you like this…sweaty and a little grimy.
No make-up.'

The flutters increased in Orla's belly. She preferred
him like this too. All elemental and wild. A man of
nature. The distance between reality and this place increased tenfold.

He pulled her over to him and she went willingly.
He lifted her so that her legs straddled his hips and she
could feel him pushing against her body. When they
kissed, it felt deep enough to drown in.

Antonio put out a hand to pull Orla up from the rock a
short while later. His chest felt tight. The sun had already turned her hair more russet and golden. Freckles
had exploded across her nose and cheeks. No make-up.
Skin shiny from suncream. Creased and dust-stained
vest top and shorts. He couldn't believe that she'd will-

ingly come on this hike with him today; she'd jumped at it. And she was the most beautiful creature he'd ever seen in his life.

He'd only just managed to pull back from stripping off her shorts and taking her right here, like two primal animals. Arousal was heavy in his body.

She stood up and glanced at him with that half-belligerent look that said, *What?* She was still grouchy from being pulled back from the brink. He smiled and he realised that he'd probably smiled more with this woman than he had…perhaps in his whole life.

An impulse came to him then and he acted on it before he could think about it. 'I want to show you something.'

'OK.'

Antonio's chest went tighter. *OK.* Just that. No moaning about dusk drawing in or the fact that she had to be tired and hot and sweaty.

Before he could change his mind, Antonio pulled Orla through a gap in the nearby bushes, until they emerged into another clearing. She stood beside him on the bluff. This had another equally stunning vista out over Saint-Raphaël, and he felt Orla's hand squeeze his. 'It's beautiful.'

Antonio knew that he could very easily just pretend that he wanted to show her the view. But he wanted to tell her. 'Do you see that long low building down there?'

He pointed to a building almost covered over with trees. Orla shaded her eyes, brought her view back into the land. She pointed too. 'The place that looks like a monastery…or a convent?'

It had a church steeple on one end.

'Yes, that's it. I bought it about a year ago.'

'Oh…OK. Why?'

Antonio deliberately kept his gaze from hers; he could feel her looking at him. 'I want to open it, as a centre to help rehabilitate soldiers after their experiences at war…in conflict zones. It needs a lot of work though, as I'd like it to double up as a medical facility for physiotherapy rehab too. It'll be a couple of years before it's even close to functional.'

Orla was quiet and Antonio was grateful. He'd noticed her glancing at his patchwork of scars at various moments, but she'd said nothing. Most of his other lovers seemed to have a desire to know the lurid details when he knew they would get sick into their designer handbags if he told them the true facts.

Eventually she said huskily, 'It's a beautiful place for such a facility.'

He stared down at her and almost lost his footing; her eyes were like sapphires. 'Yes…it is.'

To his intense relief she didn't ask any more about it and Antonio felt a little light-headed. He'd bought it out of gut instinct. A desire to help others when he'd struggled alone to cope with his own demons in the aftermath of walking away from the Legion.

'Come on…we should head back before it gets too dark.'

Just before Antonio turned, Orla squeezed his hand again.

'Thanks…for showing me.'

Antonio pulled her from the bluff before she could see how off-centre he felt.

Much later that evening, after they'd returned from the arduous hike and showered together which had inevitably led to spending even more time in the shower, they were sitting outside on the terrace near the pool, drinking wine. Orla looked at Antonio and his face was turned away, giving her his strong and patrician profile. So proud.

The urge to know about him was almost overwhelming. 'Why did you leave, in the end?'

She saw him tense, predictably. He turned his face to hers. He was wearing a white shirt that was haphazardly buttoned, showing the magnificence of his broad chest. Shorts. Hair messy and overlong.

'The Legion?'

Orla nodded and realised that he could have thought she was asking about his family too. She was suddenly ravenous for knowledge about him.

Antonio waited for the inevitable sense of intrusion to come, whenever anyone probed into this subject. Especially women. But it didn't. He sensed again that Orla wasn't the same. That she genuinely wanted to know and that she wasn't interested in the superficial. Antonio almost cursed her then for not being like that. It would be easier if she were.

However, he found it surprisingly easy to start talking. There was something incredibly peaceful just sitting with her like this. He took a breath. 'We were on a mission in Afghanistan. I was a commander of the parachute regiment. We were dropped behind enemy lines in the mountains and we found out too late that our intel was flawed. We were surrounded by rebels. Once they knew we were elite legionnaires, we became a high-priority target.

'Miraculously they weren't very well organised, and

my men managed to escape, but only because I stayed behind as a decoy.'

Antonio wasn't looking at Orla but he could sense her tensing.

'They held me captive for a month. They tortured me almost out of sheer boredom more than anything else, wanting information. Angry that the others had got away. My men managed to launch an attack and freed me the night before they'd told me I was going to be executed.'

Antonio heard Orla's breath quickening; he saw her fingers go white around the stem of her glass of wine.

'The torture was unbearable…of course. It sent me a little mad.'

Antonio knew that was an understatement. He could still recall the looks on his men's faces when they'd finally recovered him. One man had vomited.

'The circular marks on your chest?'

He nodded. 'Cigarette burns among other things. I was in hospital for nearly four months, recuperating.'

Orla's voice was almost hopeful. 'And that's when you left?'

Antonio shook his head, smiled, but it was mirthless. Because of course that was when he should have left. 'No, I went back.' Because he'd had to prove to himself that he could. Fighting the demons that would eventually overpower him.

'I left after another year, and was eventually diagnosed with PTSD. I'd been having increasingly severe panic attacks…not knowing what it was.'

'Post-traumatic stress disorder…'

He nodded again. 'I came here to this place. Marie-Ange and Dominic probably saved my life. They tended to me, made sure I had food. Dominic is ex-military and he knew what I was going through. He was the one who insisted on me seeing a therapist…and I found Tobias in London. He saved my life too.'

Antonio took a deep breath. 'I've been lucky. I have no permanent physical damage apart from a few scars. The mental damage was worse. There are those much less fortunate than me who are led to believe that nothing is wrong with them. That's why I want to open a place…for people to be able to go, free of charge. It'll be a charitable organisation.'

Orla said nothing for a long time and then Antonio heard her stand up. He couldn't look at her. He felt broken. Dirty.

She came into his line of vision though, where he couldn't ignore her, and put two hands on the arms of his chair and bent down, face close to his, eyes glittering like precious gems. And then she just pressed a kiss to his mouth. Sweet and not asking for more. But like an inferno, need swept up inside Antonio, so much that he shook with it.

Still without saying anything, Orla just stood up and held out her hand. Feeling as if something momentous was happening that he couldn't quite grasp, Antonio put his hand in hers and let her lead him upstairs. When they came together in bed, it was all the more profound because of Orla's silence. Antonio couldn't help but feel as if she'd helped cleanse something inside him. As if her silence held a wealth of compassion and understanding about something that she couldn't even possibly know, but just *did*.

When Antonio woke, it was to find himself alone in bed. He was immediately awake and immediately aware that Orla wasn't near him. It was a sixth sense that seemed to have become honed and developed in just the past few days.

Antonio dropped his head back to the pillow. He felt…curiously light. And then he recalled what he'd told Orla, and that he'd showed her the property yesterday.

What was it about her that so easily slipped under his guard? But even now he couldn't truly analyse that. All he could see was an image from the other day—Orla and Marie-Ange in bikinis splashing in the sea with the children. The way Orla had had Lily on her hip and had gently ducked her in and out of the water, as the little girl had clung to her and squealed with delight, had made something in Antonio's gut clench.

A very alien yearning for something he'd never even dared to think about stole over Antonio now, in his half wakefulness, before rationale could stamp it out. A yearning for a life. An existence. A normality he'd never known.

Just then he heard a soft noise and glanced up to see Orla in the doorway of the bedroom looking fresh and awake. Dressed in shorts and a halter-neck top. Pert breasts pushing against the fabric provocatively. Immediately, Antonio's body stirred and he growled softly, 'Come here.'

She didn't move though, and her face was serious. A trickle of foreboding went down Antonio's spine.

Orla held up her mobile phone. 'I just spoke to my father. He's back in London and wondering where I am and trying to get a hold of you. I didn't tell him that I was here with you. I have to get home, today.'

For a long second Antonio just looked at her. And

then the full magnitude of what she'd said and her serious demeanour burst into his head and spread through his body, making him feel clammy and cold. Exposed. Dousing desire.

He'd forgotten. Everything. Even the text he'd received from Lucilla only a couple of days ago: Gaining control of Kennedy Group still our priority. Please don't lose focus now. x L.

He'd lost focus. And yet clearly Orla hadn't. Even now she was moving to the wardrobe to pull out her case. Something hot and black rose up inside Antonio to see her preparing to go home without any further ado, but he pushed it down, aware of that sense of exposure eating his insides.

Instead he pushed the bedcovers aside and stood up, pulling on his jeans. He said coolly, 'I'll call the pilot and get the plane ready.'

Orla let out a shuddering breath as soon as she heard Antonio leave the room. Her eyes stung with tears. She'd been downstairs, preparing a very rudimentary breakfast, humming a tuneless song, daydreaming about what they might do that day, after a long morning spent in bed…feeling all soft and tender inside after what Antonio had told her last night. And then she'd nearly jumped out of her skin when her phone had rung.

She'd even forgotten that she'd left her phone on a side table and had been surprised that the battery hadn't died. That was how little she'd cared about being contactable. How little she'd cared about her work. And it had been her father, wondering incredulously where she was.

For someone who had never rebelled, Orla had felt

like a teenager right then. The outside world and all its responsibilities had slammed into her gut like a freight train. Her whole life had been spent focused on one thing: the family business.

But when her father had asked her where she was, the only thing that had risen up inside Orla had been resentment. Resentment that something was intruding on this sensual idyll.

When Orla had heard herself woodenly assuring her father she'd be home later that day, she'd had to come to terms with the fact that she'd woven a fantasy out of nothing. A fantasy out of a hot affair with the man who wanted to take over their business. For heaven's sake, she'd even been imagining herself here, with a child! Envying Marie-Ange for her air of domestic bliss, her beautiful kids.

She'd lost herself completely. Forgotten who she was. Thought for a minute that she could be someone else. That she could have a different life.

And worse…thought that she'd fallen in love with Antonio Chatsfield. When she'd woken that morning, she'd spent long minutes just looking at him. Her heart feeling full enough to burst.

To recall that now was the worst humiliation of all. Was she so starved of male company and sex that she fell for the first man who offered her some?

As if someone like Antonio could ever really offer her anything; he had effectively cut himself off from his entire family. He was a man who had seen and experienced the worst this world had to offer. He might have been dealing with his demons very effectively but she could see that they lurked not far behind his dark, dark eyes.

And he was clearly committed to one thing right now: the takeover for his sister's sake. Orla didn't doubt that he must hope that by doing this, he'd find a way back into his family after all these years. No wonder it was so important.

Antonio Chatsfield was the most self-contained person she'd ever met. He didn't need anyone. Had she really thought that she could be the one to soothe his soul? How many women before her had wanted that and tried? God, she was such a cliché!

Orla tried to reassure herself fiercely that she hadn't fallen for him as she dashed away the tears. She *hadn't*. It was just hormones. But the assertion sank into a very hollow spot inside her. The sooner she put this whole experience behind her, the sooner she'd be back on track, where she belonged. Building their business from the ground up again.

So why, when her business was her life, did that prospect make her feel so empty and bleak?

Orla heard Antonio's return into the room behind her and tensed. She wasn't ready to see him. She felt raw. Exposed. Humiliated. Stupid.

Anger rose up, with herself, and him, for making her feel so out of control. The words came rushing out before she could stop them. 'I should never have said yes to coming here.'

She could almost sense his tension behind her. 'What's that supposed to mean?'

She shrugged minutely, not even bothering to fold her clothes which told of her agitation more than anything else. 'Just that—we should never have come here. It was indulgent and selfish.'

She heard Antonio moving and then he was right behind her and every little hair stood up on Orla's body. Her hands tightened around some clothes.

His voice was low and definitely angry. 'Do I need to remind you that you took all of five minutes to decide to be indulgent and selfish? I didn't have to twist your arm, sweetheart.'

Something pierced Orla to hear him use the same tone he'd used when they'd first met. She still refused to turn to face him, almost scared to. 'Well, I think it's safe to say we fulfilled our remit, and now it's time to leave. Past time. We've forgotten our priorities.'

Big hands were on her shoulders and then she was being whirled around to face Antonio and her heart palpitated painfully. He was bare-chested, and she was aware of his jeans clinging sexily to those lean hips. His eyes were like blazing coals and their feral heat seared her alive.

'Fulfilled the remit? I should have realised that this exists somewhere on a chart for you of things to check off a list. Your weekly progress report.'

Orla gasped, but before she could say a word, his mouth was covering hers and he was stealing her words. Orla fought against the way her body just wanted to go up in flames.

She bunched her hands to fists against his broad chest. She tensed up. But he was too skilful—his mouth was like a torture device of pleasure. Moving against hers, his rough tongue stroking, teasing. All of the sudden and intense anger that had blown up was fading, treacherously.

He pulled back, breathing harshly, eyes almost burning her alive. 'You say we forgot our priorities? Well, you might have, but I never did. This was always about getting you where I wanted you.'

Before Orla could respond or even acknowledge the incredible pain that seemed to twist her heart in her chest, Antonio's mouth was driving down onto hers again, so passionately bruising that she had no defence for it.

She growled her frustration deep in her throat but now Antonio was stripping off her shorts and top and Orla's brain turned to heat. He laid her down on the bed and stripped off his own jeans.

Electricity crackled between them. Sanity tried to break through; Orla struggled up on her elbows but Antonio was lying beside her now, his hand roving down her belly, under her panties, fingers seeking and finding where she seemed to be perpetually aroused. For him.

Gutturally he said, 'This is why we came here, Orla. For no other reason.'

Equally gutturally, Orla replied with a fierceness that shocked her. 'Then this is it.' She didn't have to elaborate. *After this—it's over.*

He just looked at her and she couldn't decipher the expression on his face but it was as fierce as her words, spoken and unspoken. And then he just said, 'Yes.'

Orla tried to stifle a sob that seemed to erupt from deep within her, just as his fingers moved within her and his mouth fastened over the tight bud of her nipple. She masked the sob of emotion as a sob of need. Orla despaired that she didn't have the strength to push him away and say no.

And when Antonio moved over her body, pinning her hands over her head with one of his, she could do nothing but arch her back and widen her legs around him, and bite her lip to stop from crying out when he entered her. And know that this would be the last time.

Orla was as tense as a board on the plane home. She could still feel the burn of Antonio's lovemaking between her legs. It had been so intense. Antonio's voice on the other side of the small plane cut through the numbness that seemed to have enveloped her since they'd made love and left.

'Patrick Kennedy is back in London. Yes. I'm on my way back. Set up a meeting for a week's time. That should give us both time to get everything in order.'

Orla steeled herself and looked across at Antonio to find his dark enigmatic gaze on hers. Her skin prickled with need, even now. When she knew it shouldn't.

'I'll talk to you later, David.' He put down the phone.

Orla tried to keep the bitterness out of her voice, the angry emotion she still felt to think of how this man had turned her world upside down so comprehensively. And how she'd been unable to resist him, right up until the last moment.

'So, you're all set, then?'

Antonio's mouth firmed. 'Looks like it. There's nothing to stop this deal going ahead now. I don't think you're going to say no, are you?'

In a low voice she said, 'You know I can't. I don't have a choice. It's up to my father.'

Afraid he'd hear the emotion, she forced a lighter voice. 'Your sister will be pleased to have the focus put back on how well the Chatsfield brand is doing.'

Antonio's eyes looked very dark. 'You know that's always been my main priority.'

Orla's insides curdled to hear him say that but she

forced herself to respond as lightly as possible. 'I'm sure the rest of your siblings will appreciate your help in restoring the Chatsfield brand.'

It was crazy and ridiculous to feel so betrayed by someone who was patently never going to have *her* best interests at heart. But she did. For the first time in her life. Even her father had never truly appreciated her full worth or what she did for him but it had never impacted her like this. And that revelation was…*huge*.

Orla thought of how Antonio had taken control of her mother that day and how it had made her feel and she hated him for giving her that illusion of support, protection. Unable to stem the tide of emotion rising inexorably upwards, Orla felt her eyes fill but didn't turn her head quickly enough from that incisive black gaze.

His voice was sharp. 'Orla?'

She couldn't speak. She shook her head fiercely. But then she heard him unbuckle his belt and come out of his seat. She felt him crouching down at her knees.

Humiliation and self-recrimination burned her. She'd only had to hold it together for this flight and she couldn't even do that.

'Orla?'

His hand came to her jaw, turning her to face him. Tears were running down her face now, her chest jerking in a bid to keep the sobs back. He was just a big dark blurry figure.

'Just leave me be, Antonio.' Her voice was thick.

He was shaking his head, eyes glittering. Face pale. 'What is it, Orla? *Dammit*, tell me.'

She shook her head and took his hand away from her chin. But he wouldn't move.

'What is it? The takeover?'

The anger left Orla as quickly as it had risen. She couldn't possibly be more laid bare or exposed than she was now. This man had altered her DNA and she could no more deny it than stop breathing.

She shook her head and wiped at her tears. 'No. It's… *us.*'

Antonio went very still and said nothing for a long moment. His eyes burned so fiercely that they seemed like black coals in his face.

In a hoarse voice he said, 'I didn't know.'

Ice filled Orla's veins. 'Didn't know what?' she spat out, the anger rising again for allowing herself to fall apart so spectacularly. At Antonio's stunned expression. At the confirmation that he'd felt nothing. 'Didn't know that I could be capable of changing? That within the space of a few days, I'd find myself wanting more?'

Orla wanted to look away but she couldn't. He shook his head. 'I don't…' He stopped and when he spoke again he sounded tortured. 'I *can't.*'

And suddenly Orla just felt incredibly bereft. Even as something else slid into place inside her—some very revelatory acceptance that she *had* changed on a deep level, and perhaps her priorities were different now, but that was OK.

'I've seen things, Orla…things that no human being should ever see. I've witnessed things. I've *killed* people, all in the name of fighting the good fight. And I have a family that don't even know me.'

She reached out and touched Antonio's cheek with a trembling hand. 'I know.'

He laughed but it was bitter. '*You* know me better than they do.'

But Orla took no comfort in that right now. She could

see Antonio retreating to some place she couldn't reach. She'd fallen for a man who wasn't ready to be fallen for. And the pain was excruciating. She wanted to try and plead with him to let her in, to let her show him that she could help him. But she was too scared. She'd already exposed herself more than she could bear without actually telling him she loved him.

The pilot announced that they were beginning their descent into London and Orla's heart broke in two. Antonio, still at her feet, just looked at her with a wealth of unfathomable pain in his eyes and said, 'I'm sorry.'

All she could say was a quiet 'Me too.'

And then Antonio got up and sat back down and buckled his belt and Orla flinched at the sound. She felt wrung out and empty.

When they emerged from the plane, Orla sent up silent thanks that she'd had the foresight to ask her assistant, Susan, to arrange a car for her.

She put her bag in the back and turned to see Antonio standing feet away, just watching her. He walked over to her and with every step Orla's heart pumped harder. Maybe, just maybe—

He slid his hand under her hair, around the back of her neck. Her entire body prickled. Waiting. And then he just said in a rough voice, 'Goodbye, Orla.'

And then he took his hand away and he was turning, striding, disappearing into the back of his own car. And then, gone.

Orla wanted to run after his car, screaming and shouting. Banging on the window for him to stop. For him to not be such a coward. *Him!* She could appreciate the irony. A man who had endured torture.

And perhaps she had to realise he wasn't being a

coward at all. He just didn't feel as deeply as she did. And that nearly hurt more than anything.

As Antonio drove away from Orla, all he could see was her beautiful tear-stained face and hear her rough entreaty: *us*. It scored at his insides like a hot knife. With a pain worse than any torture he'd experienced.

He'd lied back in France. He'd been so incensed that she appeared to be cool and collected about going home that he'd told her he'd never lost sight of why they were there. But he had. Completely. For the first time in his life he'd lost his focus. He'd found himself on the shimmering edges of a dream that was so seductive…a dream he'd never allowed himself to come close to before.

Orla's tears had opened up a million wounds inside Antonio. Wounds that he'd spent painstaking time covering up, healing over. He felt held together by a patchwork of scars as it was.

That one word, *us*, had gone off like a bomb inside him. Threatening everything in its wake. He didn't know if he could be torn apart and built up again. It had happened already and he'd almost died.

Antonio felt a sense of desolation rise through him, the like of which he'd never experienced, not even when their mother had left them all those years ago. He felt tainted, bruised. Warped. Damaged. How could he seize a dream when he'd turned his back on it so long ago?

# CHAPTER NINE

'LUCILLA? *DAMMIT.*' ANTONIO cursed and cut off the connection again when the automated voice came back: *The person you are trying to reach may be out of coverage or have their phone powered off.*

What was going on with his sister anyway? Antonio had only had the briefest and most cryptic of messages from her saying something garbled about having to leave England for a few days and that he should do whatever he thought best with regards to the hotel takeover.

*Whatever was best?* Antonio's mouth twisted. Whatever was best for him was to walk away and forget he had ever heard the name Kennedy. And in particular, *Orla Kennedy.* The past week had seen Antonio grow progressively more and more irritated. Snarling at anything that moved near him. His car was stuck in horn-beeping London traffic and it was starting to rain. Matching his mood perfectly.

He'd not slept all week. His nights interspersed with torrid dreams and worse, nightmares of his time in the Legion. Nightmares he hadn't had to battle with for over a year. It was as if he was sliding backwards into a morass of darkness.

It didn't help to acknowledge the small voice that reminded him that when Orla had shared his bed, he'd slept better than he could ever remember sleeping. After one particularly vivid nightmare only last night, Antonio had slept fitfully again only to have a tantalising dream of Orla taking him by the hand and feeling a sense of peace so profound steal over him that when he'd woken in his anonymous Chatsfield suite, he'd felt possibly lonelier than he'd ever felt in his life.

His car finally pulled up outside the London Kennedy hotel and everything in Antonio tensed, even as the chasm inside him lessened slightly. *Orla.* He would see her again. In minutes. He knew he shouldn't be relishing this sense of anticipation, but he couldn't help it. For the first time all week, that sense of peace he'd felt in his dream last night touched him again, soothing him.

Clenching his jaw as if he could deny it, Antonio got out of his car and walked into the main foyer. But as soon as he entered he knew Orla wasn't there, wasn't anywhere in the vicinity. It was immediate and visceral, that sixth sense he'd developed around her presence. He stopped in the middle of reception. Everything had a more muted air. People didn't seem to be smiling so much. It was *less*. Empty.

He saw a young buck in a uniform at the concierge desk where old Lawrence usually was. Something surged up within Antonio and he strode over to ask curtly, 'Where is Lawrence?'

The young concierge visibly gulped at the look on Antonio's face. 'Er…I believe he's out sick, sir.… Can I help?'

Something tangled and black was rising up within Antonio as he turned and went to the reception desk.

One of the junior managers recognised him and rushed over, breathless. 'Mr Chatsfield, you're early—'

Antonio all but snarled at the man. 'Has anyone thought to check up on Lawrence? To make sure he's all right?'

The manager blanched and stuttered, 'Well…no, we didn't think—'

'Well, see to it that someone is sent over to his place immediately and let me know how he is.'

The manager blanched even more. 'Yes, yes, of course. I mean, I'm sure someone has thought to—'

But Antonio had already turned away. If Orla was here it would have been the first thing she'd done. Probably going over to check on the man herself. *Dammit.* Where was she?

Just then Tom Barry appeared, the Kennedy Group solicitor. All smooth charm. 'Mr Chatsfield, if you'd like to follow me, everyone is in the conference room.'

Grim-faced, Antonio followed but he already knew what he wouldn't see when he stepped into the room. *Orla*, in one of her prissy but oh-so-sexy suits. A defiant look on her face. Her hair up and begging to be tumbled down. And that chasm in his chest expanded again.

After an hour of listening stony-faced to negotiations over the minutiae of keeping the Kennedy Group brand name intact under the Chatsfield umbrella, Antonio had had enough. Resolve firmed in his belly, and for the first time since he'd seen Orla last, he felt slightly sane again.

He stood up and everyone stopped talking. Orla's father, Patrick Kennedy, glanced up in surprise. He was an attractive ebullient-looking man but he also looked exhausted. And beaten.

Antonio said in a tone that brooked no argument, 'I want everyone to please leave, except for Mr Kennedy and our two solicitors.'

When everyone had filed out, Antonio sat down again and addressed Orla's father. 'Sir, if I may speak frankly?'

Orla's father nodded, hesitant.

'The fact is, I don't really give a damn about whether or not we take you over any more. But I do give a damn about something else, and that's what I'd like to discuss.'

Orla was on her hands and knees under the desk in her office which held the printer, fax machine and a myriad assortment of equipment. She cursed volubly when the plug wouldn't go where it should.

'Mary,' she called out, 'I think we need to get Brian the spark back in. There's another dodgy plug here.'

'I'm not a trained electrician but even I can tell you that it's not the best idea to force something into an electrical socket if it doesn't want to go.'

Orla stopped dead. *His voice.* From right behind her. The plug was still in her hand. Her whole body went cold, and then hot. It couldn't be. She was dreaming him up during the day now, as well as the long empty nights.

Cursing herself for this treacherous hallucination and fully expecting to see their handyman or one of the suppliers behind her, Orla emerged out from under the desk and slowly straightened up. And turned around.

Antonio stood in the small modest office, effort-lessly dominating the space. Dressed in a dark suit and light shirt. Hair thick and unruly. Jaw unshaven. Utterly masculine, utterly gorgeous. Orla blinked. She felt nothing. But she was dimly aware that her numbness was shock and it was holding a veritable flood of emotion and physical reactions at bay.

Somehow she managed to speak. 'What are you doing here?'

His eyes were intense on her. Black. 'The terms of the agreement with your father have changed.'

Orla automatically glanced at her mobile phone on the nearby table and reached over to press a button. No calls. She looked back up; sensations were starting to break through the numbness. Incredible hurt. Pain. *Desire*.

'I haven't heard from him.'

'Because I asked him to let me come and tell you in person.'

Orla could feel reaction making her limbs turn to jelly. She crossed her arms. 'So you came all the way to one of the remotest parts of Ireland to pass on this information? What game are you playing, Antonio? I would have thought all the *i*'s were dotted, and *t*'s crossed by now.'

His face was implacable. 'Why weren't you in London to see the deal through with your father?'

Orla blanched and avoided his eye. There was something almost accusing in his tone. She wasn't about to tell him of her resolve not to be a part of the signing of the deal because she hadn't been able to bear the thought of facing him across that table again. Cold, remote. After everything that had happened.

She looked back. 'Because I decided it was best to come here to get a head start on renovations for this hotel.' Her mouth went into a bitter line. 'There was no need for me at the London end—everything was in place to sign off our business…which I presume is now done?'

But Antonio shook his head slowly. 'No, Orla, it's not done. At least, not the way you think. We did sign an agreement, but now you still own the hotel in New York, and the ones in London, and Dublin.'

Orla felt the blood drain from her face. 'But…what? How?'

Antonio's expression became enigmatic, unreadable. 'Because we proposed a new deal to your father. We've decided to become investors…and he's agreed to sell off all his remaining assets in favour of his main flagship hotels. Thus giving the Kennedy Group a chance to regenerate.'

Orla couldn't stay standing; she felt for the chair behind her and sat down weakly. Antonio's eyes narrowed on her and he cursed softly. Just then a matronly woman appeared and her eyes widened to see this virile specimen of manliness in the office.

Orla could have laughed at Mary's expression if she'd been able to breathe. Antonio rapped out, 'Can you bring us some brandy?'

Mary blinked and glanced at Orla and then rushed off, clearly seeing the need for the drink. Orla looked at Antonio, who stayed standing.

He spoke her whirling thoughts out loud. His voice disturbingly soft. 'It's your plan, Orla. What you wanted to happen. A chance to save the group.'

She shook her head. Was she dreaming? She wanted to pinch herself but then Mary was bustling back with a tumbler of brandy and handing it to Orla. Mary disappeared again and pulled the door behind her. Orla took a swift sip, her hand trembling slightly. The drink burned her throat and settled in her stomach, steadying warmth radiating outwards.

Antonio didn't disappear. She wasn't dreaming.

'But how? Why?' She couldn't seem to string a sentence together.

Antonio started to pace back and forth as if standing still too long was caging him in like an animal.

'Our priorities have changed. We're no longer interested in a takeover. Investment in a viable successful business is more attractive to us right now.'

Orla stared at Antonio suspiciously. There was something off about his words…and yet he was here, in her office, in the deepest part of the west of Ireland. Why would he have come all this way? Her heart sped up but she refused to even go there mentally.

He stopped and pinned her with his black gaze. It dropped momentarily and Orla's breath hitched. She became acutely aware of her black silk shirt and black skirt. Dammit. She must look like some kind of a widow in mourning. But when she'd left London last week she'd thrown all the clothes she'd worn in France into the back of her wardrobe and had pulled out her most severe work clothes.

'You need to come back to London with me.'

Panic seized Orla's innards at the thought of going anywhere with this man. She shook her head, stood up again. 'No, I need to stay here and get the hotel ready for refurbishment.'

A familiar steeliness came over Antonio's features and Orla's belly quivered.

'Did you hear anything I just said? The deal is off. We've got a new deal. One that keeps the Kennedy Group afloat.' His jaw clenched. 'But I'm not signing the final papers until you witness them.'

'Antonio…' Even just saying his name made Orla feel dizzy.

'I have a plane waiting at Kerry Airport.'

She opened her mouth again but he shook his head. 'Either you come with me now, Orla, or this deal is off and you'll be left with nothing.'

At last, something she could cling on to when it felt as if the world had gone mad. Orla straightened her spine. 'What is it about you Chatsfields? Do you get your kicks from playing with people as if they're little beetles running around a chessboard?'

His eyes flashed and to Orla's chagrin it looked as if one corner of his mouth tipped up slightly. He was laughing at her! Galvanised, Orla marched around the desk to stand in front of him, putting her hands on her hips.

'If you think that you can just barge in here—'

The half-smile faded from his mouth. 'Did you know that Lawrence was in hospital?'

Immediately Orla's ire melted away, replaced with shock and concern. 'No! What's wrong with him? How do you know? What happened?'

It was only when Antonio was explaining about sending someone to check on him and that they'd found him collapsed in his home that Orla realised he'd somehow manoeuvred her so that she was now in the back of his car, with her bag on her lap, and they were driving away from the hotel which looked out over the stormy Atlantic sea.

Her eyes snapped back to Antonio. 'Of all the rotten, manipulative—'

Antonio sat back looking smug. But even now Orla couldn't rest until she knew for sure. 'Is he being looked after?'

Antonio nodded. 'By my own physician. He wasn't feeling well, and then he had a fall at home. Nothing is broken, but he needs to be monitored. It could be the end of his time at the hotel though.'

Orla felt a sadness that was disproportionate to her affection for the old man. Guilt lanced her. How could she be feeling sorrier for herself when the culprit of her pain was right beside her and confusing her with his behaviour?

She didn't like how Antonio's obvious concern for their aged employee made her feel soft inside. Tender. Vulnerable.

The air seemed to grow thick between them. Heavy with unspoken things and physical awareness. Orla's hands literally itched to reach out and place them somewhere, anywhere, on his body.

She looked away from temptation, out the window at the familiar green countryside, and stayed tense enough to break until they arrived at Kerry Airport, where a small jet was waiting.

He seemed determined to furnish her with no more information until they got to London and so Orla stayed quiet too, afraid of what might come out of her mouth if she opened it. Afraid of what had come out the last time.

When they arrived in London, another car was waiting for them and whisked them into the city. Orla battled déjà vu to think of the similar journey last week when she'd felt so empty and desolate. Now she felt as if her nerves were too sensitive after being in the relative peace and solitude of the west of Ireland.

Just then she noticed that they weren't going in the right direction for the hotel, or his. They were heading in the opposite direction.

'Hey...' She turned to Antonio, eyes narrowed. 'Where are we going?'

He actually looked nervous and Orla reeled. She didn't think that Antonio Chatsfield would even understand the concept of being nervous, never mind *look* it. 'We're taking a small diversion.'

Orla felt nervous herself now. Butterflies jumping around her belly. She could see that they were in and around the upmarket Notting Hill area. The butterflies increased.

Antonio's face was as impassive as a stone. She felt sick to recall how she'd confided in him about looking at houses on her days off. How he'd teased her.

They were on a wide leafy road now, dappled sunlight filtering through the trees. Tall houses on either side. It was one of Notting Hill's most exclusive streets. Antonio's car pulled up outside an elegant four-storey town house, steps leading up to a classy dark blue front door. Mentally, Orla was already repainting it a rich dark grey.

Her insides were jumping around, a knot in her belly. She looked at Antonio, a question in her eyes. He just said, 'Bear with me, a few minutes longer.'

He got out of the car and came around and opened Orla's door, putting out a hand. Orla hesitated for a few seconds before allowing herself to touch him. A shiver of longing went through her body when his big hand enclosed hers.

He pulled her out and led her up the steps. To her surprise he had a key and opened the door, leading her in. Stunned, Orla followed him into the long ornately tiled hall, off which were two huge reception rooms. The rooms were empty, clearly waiting for someone— *new owners?*—to fill them with furniture.

A ball of emotion was growing in Orla's chest. She was afraid to look at Antonio and so she let him lead her around silently, showing her the huge kitchen-cum-den area in the basement which led out through French doors to a beautiful landscaped garden stretching all the way back to a small copse of trees.

In the basement there was also a gym and a vast utility area. And a playroom. Upstairs there were five bedrooms and an attic space that could be used as an office or another bedroom. Numerous bathrooms. The stunning master bedroom had a palatial en-suite bathroom and two dressing rooms attached. It was also empty but for a massive undressed bed. Orla flushed when she saw it, her hand going immediately sweaty in Antonio's, but when she tried to pull away he wouldn't let her.

When they came back down to the reception rooms, Orla was feeling shaky. She finally took her hand from his and stood back, feeling wobbly. 'What is this, Antonio?'

'I need to clarify something I said earlier…before we go any further.'

Orla just looked at him.

Taking a deep breath, Antonio told her, 'When I told you that *we*, meaning the Chatsfields, had decided to invest in the Kennedy Group rather than take it over, it wasn't entirely accurate.'

Orla crossed her arms over her chest, battling the simmering butterflies in her gut.

'The more accurate version is that it's a personal

investment from me. I was afraid if you knew you wouldn't come with me.'

Orla's arms tightened, and she gasped. 'You? Alone?'

He nodded. She was stunned. 'But...why? What about your sister? What about improving the Chatsfield brand?'

Antonio's mouth firmed and Orla had to stop her mind from straying to wanting to feel that mouth on hers.

'The truth is that I took an executive decision to do this myself. My sister is incommunicado, but I'll deal with her when she reappears, and if she still wants to take over a hotel chain I'm sure there are plenty of others I can steer her towards.'

Orla was feeling increasingly disorientated. 'But... why?' she asked again.

Antonio's eyes were dark. 'Because I know how much it means to you. Because, to be quite frank, the Kennedy Group ethos doesn't exist without you there. And apart from that, it's a very viable business investment. The Kennedy Group has the potential to grow once again and become even stronger than it ever was, in the right hands. Your father has increased your shares so that you have equal, if not more, say than he does in the day-to-day running of things.'

Orla blanched.

Antonio sounded grim. 'It was part of the deal, that you had to have more power.'

The thought that this man had laid that out, when her own father had never seen fit to acknowledge her role, made her feel ridiculously vulnerable and exposed. Still reeling, Orla asked a little belligerently, 'And what's your stake in it all?'

Antonio's face took on a stern regard. 'Forty per cent.'

Orla's belly quivered. 'So we would be…partners.'

He nodded. 'Yes. As any investor would have been.'

Orla felt constricted all of a sudden, the thought of Antonio being in her day-to-day life, for the foreseeable future…that he'd had the temerity to go behind her back and seek more power for her—it was too much to take in.

She backed away a little, terrified of the direction her wayward thoughts wanted to travel, down dangerous roads, flights of fancy. 'You really think that it's a good idea that we work together? You left your own family business behind a long time ago….'

Her mouth pursed. She had to stop herself from reminding him that only a few days ago they'd said *goodbye* and yet this would mean…the opposite. She couldn't even let her mind grasp that right now. It was too dangerous.

'Pardon me if I fail to believe that you suddenly want to immerse yourself in that world again.'

Antonio's jaw clenched. A muscle throbbed. 'Ask me why I'm showing you this house, Orla.'

Suddenly Orla didn't want to. It felt like the most loaded question in the universe. But Antonio was a huge immovable force. And she refused to show him how intimidated she was.

She steeled herself. Pretending like she didn't care what his answer would be. 'Why are you showing me this house?'

He was quiet for a long time and then he finally said, 'Because…I want to buy it for you.'

Hope flared so bright inside Orla that she felt dizzy before she clamped down on it ruthlessly. He was just playing with her. And she'd unwittingly given him the key to the most vulnerable part of her. He just *wanted* her, nothing more.

Unable to keep a slight tremor of emotion from her voice and hating herself for it, Orla said, 'You know, most men give a woman a diamond bracelet or flowers. This is taking it a bit far, don't you think? After all, we were only together for, what? Two, three weeks? Or maybe you want to set me up in some convenient location?'

Antonio's eyes flashed and his jaw tightened, but he just said, 'Do you like the house, Orla?'

The ball of emotion got bigger in her chest. Getting angry now, she answered, 'Do I like the house?'

She threw her arms open, feeling prickly, vulnerable and reckless. 'This house is my dream come to life! Is that it, Antonio? You're not quite finished showing me how easily you can dominate my life? Now you want to set me up so you can come and go as you please?'

His eyes flashed again but with something far more ambiguous this time. Something hot. Biting her lip, Orla turned away, her eyes prickling ominously.

From behind her she heard him say, 'I want to buy this house for you.'

She couldn't face him again. Tears were starting to fill her eyes in earnest now. This was torture. Swallowing the lump the size of her throat, she said thickly, 'That's really not necessary, Antonio. I can buy my own house if I really want to and I have no interest in becoming a mistress—'

He cut her off. 'But if I do buy the house for you it comes with a condition.'

Her heart was aching. 'Antonio, like I said, I really don't want to—'

*'The condition is that I come with the house.'*

She stopped dead. Her heart thumped. Had she just heard…? She turned around slowly, vision slightly blurry. Antonio had that look on his face again. Nervous.

'What did you just say?'

He came closer and she couldn't move.

'I said, if I buy this house…it comes with me attached. Because I want to live here with you.'

His mouth twisted. 'I don't want you as my mistress. I want to create a life together. Because this past week is the last time that I want to spend more than a night apart from you.'

Orla wasn't breathing. She could only see two pools of dark brown. Glowing. Intense.

'Because,' he continued, 'I love you, Orla Kennedy, and I don't want to be rootless any more. I knew I loved you last week but I was the biggest emotional coward on this earth and I couldn't face up to it. Quite simply, I'd prefer to endure the torture I did when I was a soldier, for the rest of my life, rather than spend another moment without you, because without you I feel as if I'm unravelling at the seams.'

His words washed through her and sank in slowly. His gaze was unwavering, speaking volumes. She saw it in his eyes. The emotion Orla had locked away in her gut broke free, spreading outwards, obliterating doubt and fear in its path.

She bridged the gap between them, curling her hands around the lapels of Antonio's jacket, the heat of his body surrounding her, telling her that she wasn't dreaming. She looked up at him and said huskily, 'What took you so damn long, Chatsfield?'

He was serious. 'What took me so long is that I'm terrified, of the things I've seen and done. I know that something broke inside me a long time ago, and it was only when I was with you that I started to feel whole again. But I'm scared too...of the darkness.'

Orla felt dizzy with the tenderness rushing through her. She put her hand to Antonio's cheek, feeling the bristle of his stubble against the tender skin of her palm.

'If you'll let me...I'll help you. We can do this together. You deserve happiness, Antonio. You deserve to lay those ghosts to rest and to live a life.'

Her heart clenched tight when she saw the brightness in his eyes.

'That's what I want. A life, with you.'

Orla reached up and pressed a kiss to his mouth, her heart overflowing. 'Then you have it, my love.'

She saw his expression change, felt his body tighten. 'You love me?'

She smiled but could have wept at the insecurity in his eyes. 'In case it's not completely obvious, I fell for you somewhere along the way between that first night and right now. And I'm still falling for you.' Simply, with quiet fervent conviction, she said, 'I love you.'

Antonio's hands framed Orla's face; they were shaking. 'Thank God. I love you so much.... This week was...'

Orla turned her head and pressed a kiss to Antonio's palm and covered his hand with hers. She looked up into his eyes, emotion making her voice thick as she finished for him. 'Agony.'

Antonio emitted something guttural, elemental, and

then his mouth was on hers, passionate and bruising, and Orla matched it. Stretching up, twining her arms around his neck, pressing as close as she could.

Desire exploded between them. Antonio broke away to say roughly, 'I sacrificed my youth for my family and it ruined my relationship with my father and my brothers and sisters. And then I ran as far away as I could… and I didn't stop running until I laid eyes on you. I've ached for you…my whole life.'

Shakily she said, 'I was running too, away from myself.… I need you so much.'

Tears filled Orla's eyes and Antonio saw them and looked panicked. 'Don't cry. Please. When you cried last week, it nearly killed me.'

Orla managed a watery smile. 'Then hurry up and do something to distract me.'

Sounding grim, Antonio said, 'The bed…upstairs.'

He was already tugging Orla from the room and excitement made her blood hum with anticipation, even as something struck her. 'But what if someone comes?'

Antonio glanced back and looked mildly sheepish. 'They won't. I took a gamble and already bought the house.'

Orla's heart leapt but she feigned indignance as he pulled her into the master bedroom. 'And what if I'd said I hated the house?'

Antonio stopped and turned to face Orla, taking her face in his hands again. 'Then I would have kept buying houses and showing them to you until you found the one you liked.'

Breathless, because Antonio was taking off his jacket and his hands were on her shirt now, Orla said, 'That's not very economical in these straitened times.'

Antonio said something rude about the economy and stripped off Orla's shirt, his cheeks flushing to see her lace-covered breasts. He looked at her, slightly tortured for a moment, and he cursed. 'I wanted to do this properly, but I look at you and I forget…'

He got down on one knee then and Orla's heart leapt, *again*. At this rate she was close to having a heart attack. He found his jacket and pulled a box from a pocket. A small velvet box.

He gazed up at her and opened the box to reveal a beautiful solitaire diamond ring set in a wide band of smaller diamonds.

'Orla Kate Kennedy…will you please marry me?'

Too shocked and stunned and overcome to cry, Orla just nodded stupidly…finally managing to say huskily, 'Yes, Antonio Marco Chatsfield, I'll marry you.'

Antonio pushed the ring onto Orla's finger, where it glittered brilliantly, but she was too intent on getting Antonio back where she wanted him to inspect it. She pulled him up and pressed her mouth to his, revelling in his hands moving over her, divesting her of her clothes, and his, until they were both naked and fell in a tangle of bronzed and pale limbs, onto the bed.

Orla thought of something and speared her fingers in Antonio's hair, dragging his head back up from her breast. They were both breathless. 'Do you mind if I don't change my name?'

Antonio frowned. 'Why would I mind if you didn't change your name?'

Orla smiled. 'I like the sound of Kennedy-Chatsfield.'

Antonio smiled too. 'Maybe I'll change *my* name.'

Orla rolled her eyes. 'Just the thing to welcome your family back into your life.'

Sounding a little hoarse, Antonio said, 'What's that supposed to mean?'

Orla's hands cupped his face. 'It means that I'm here for you no matter what. And sooner or later you're going to get in touch with your brothers and sisters and let them know you're back.'

Orla could see the emotion in his eyes. How much it meant to him to hear her say that. He pressed a kiss to her mouth, soft, lingering. And then Orla moved over him so that she lay sprawled over his body, her thighs either side of his hips, the heart of her body almost touching the head of his erection.

Antonio felt emotion obliterating the last vestiges of darkness inside him.

This was the last bastion, the image he'd never really allowed himself to even envisage, believing himself to be too dark and twisted inside.

He pushed some vibrant red hair over her pale shoulder and pressed a kiss there before gazing deep into those sapphire eyes. His chest expanded and before he could say anything Orla put a finger to his lips, and with her eyes shining suspiciously bright, she said, 'Yes, at least two. A boy and a girl, but I don't really care about that as long as they're healthy and look like you….'

They shared a look of such communion and intensity Antonio felt as if he'd come just from looking at her, but before he did, he joined their bodies and showed her without words all of the emotion in his heart, for her.

# EPILOGUE

*Three years later*

'DA-DA-DA-DA-DA-DA!'

Orla gave up trying to keep a hold of her wriggling eighteen-month-old daughter, Ashling, when she reacted with predictable glee to seeing her favourite person in the world.

She smiled wryly at the padded bottom waddling in her cute romper suit as the sturdy body fell headlong into the safe hands of her adoring father.

For a second Orla's breath caught when she saw the two identically dark-haired heads together, and then Ashling broke away from sloppily kissing her father's big grin to look at her mother with huge innocent dark blue eyes as if to apologise for being so blatantly disloyal.

Orla stood up from where she'd been playing with Ashling on the lawn outside the villa and strolled towards her husband, her blood heating as it always did when his eyes seemed to devour her even after only a short absence. In this case, a pathetic couple of hours.

He bent and pressed a lingering kiss to her mouth,

ignoring Ashling's shameless attempts to gain his attention by clapping her chubby hands in front of his face.

Luckily Marie-Ange appeared then from the side of the house with Lily, and Ashling's attention was diverted and she wriggled to be put down to chase after her second-favourite person. She hero-worshipped Lily.

Antonio obliged and watched her toddle off, only turning back when he knew she was safe.

Orla took advantage of the undoubtedly brief moment of peace to snake her arms around Antonio's waist. She revelled in his equally possessive hold and pressed close to his body.

He looked down at her and arched a brow, mock-chagrin on his face at her wry expression. 'What? I can't help it if my daughter finds me as irresistible as her mother does.'

Orla grumbled good-naturedly, 'Just wait till we have a son. Then you'll know all about favourites.

'Marie-Ange has been cooking up a storm all day. And I've been helping but I'm afraid she's told me to leave the kitchen in case I set it on fire again with my enthusiastic flambéing. "Baby steps," she keeps saying.'

Orla saw Antonio smile and felt emotion surge because there was no trepidation or doubt in his eyes any more. They were due an influx of visitors tomorrow—his family. It was becoming an annual pilgrimage.

It had taken a while for him to feel comfortable around his brothers and sisters again, the weight of guilt a heavy thing to throw off overnight. But getting to know them again had helped.

It hadn't been easy, yet over the years Antonio had

begun to develop a strong relationship with his father, who had even apologised to Antonio for being so hard on him.

Antonio twirled some of Orla's hair around his finger. 'You're a force to be reckoned with, you know that, Mrs Kennedy-Chatsfield? And I couldn't care less that you can't cook a boiled egg without burning the water.'

And then more seriously Orla asked, 'How was it?'

Antonio tucked the lock of hair he'd been playing with behind her ear and said, 'Good. The physiotherapy unit is ready to be opened tomorrow, and not a moment too soon with ten more soldiers due to arrive by the end of the week.'

Orla felt pride squeeze up into her throat, constricting it for a minute. Antonio's project—the Soldiers Rehabilitation Clinic, as it was now known—had opened six months previously. It was a great success with a huge waiting list already and talk of more centres being opened up.

Antonio was a different man these days, lighter. There had been a lot of healing in the past few years, for them both.

When Orla could speak, she said huskily, 'I'm so proud of you.'

Antonio shook his head, his hand cupping her jaw. 'It wouldn't exist...*I* wouldn't exist...without you.'

And then, pulling her closer, he growled softly, 'Do you think Marie-Ange will miss us if we disappear for a short while?'

Orla gave him a stern but explicit look. '*Very* short. The poor woman has been slaving over a hot stove all day.'

With that, Antonio took Orla's hand and all but dragged her into the house and they had just enough time to work on making a son before a familiar plaintive cry started up in the distance: *'Dada!'*

*  *  *  *  *

*If you enjoyed this book,
look out for the next instalment of*
THE CHATSFIELD:
*REBEL'S BARGAIN by Annie West,
coming next month.*

## #3285 THE VALQUEZ SEDUCTION
*The Playboys of Argentina*
### by Melanie Milburne
When Argentinian polo player Luiz Valquez rescues innocent Daisy Wyndham, the press reports they're engaged! It's a dangerous charade: with Luiz doing his best to be good and Daisy trying to be bad, how long before someone gives in?

## #3286 ONE NIGHT WITH MORELLI
### by Kim Lawrence
Eve Curtis is determined to remain independent and is happy keeping men at a safe distance. Until now. Because when Draco Morelli sweeps her off her feet, he opens her eyes to a whole new world of sin and seduction....

## #3287 THE RUSSIAN'S ACQUISITION
### by Dani Collins
Alesky Dmitriev's revenge plans backfire when he discovers that his new mistress, Clair Daniels, is a virgin! Undeterred, he's set on enjoying the perks of his purchase. Clair, however, is destined to be much more than just this Russian's acquisition.

## #3288 THE TRUE KING OF DAHAAR
*A Dynasty of Sand and Scandal*
### by Tara Pammi
Nikhat Zakhari's desertion once drove Prince Azeez to recklessness, but now he must choose: spend life in the shadows of the past, or embrace his future. He *must* assume the crown—but will Nikhat agree to be his desert queen?

---

HPCNM1014RB

# REQUEST YOUR FREE BOOKS!

## 2 FREE NOVELS PLUS
# 2 FREE GIFTS!

*PASSION GUARANTEED SEDUCTION*

**YES!** Please send me 2 FREE Harlequin Presents® novels and my 2 FREE gifts (gifts are worth about $10). After receiving them, if I don't wish to receive any more books, I can return the shipping statement marked "cancel." If I don't cancel, I will receive 6 brand-new novels every month and be billed just $4.30 per book in the U.S. or $4.99 per book in Canada. That's a saving of at least 14% off the cover price! It's quite a bargain! Shipping and handling is just 50¢ per book in the U.S. and 75¢ per book in Canada.* I understand that accepting the 2 free books and gifts places me under no obligation to buy anything. I can always return a shipment and cancel at any time. Even if I never buy another book, the two free books and gifts are mine to keep forever.

106/306 HDN FVRK

| | |
|---|---|
| Name | (PLEASE PRINT) |

| | |
|---|---|
| Address | Apt. # |

| | | |
|---|---|---|
| City | State/Prov. | Zip/Postal Code |

Signature (if under 18, a parent or guardian must sign)

### Mail to the **Harlequin® Reader Service:**
**IN U.S.A.:** P.O. Box 1867, Buffalo, NY  14240-1867
**IN CANADA:** P.O. Box 609, Fort Erie, Ontario  L2A 5X3

### Are you a current subscriber to Harlequin Presents books and want to receive the larger-print edition?
Call 1-800-873-8635 or visit www.ReaderService.com.

\* Terms and prices subject to change without notice. Prices do not include applicable taxes. Sales tax applicable in N.Y. Canadian residents will be charged applicable taxes. Offer not valid in Quebec. This offer is limited to one order per household. Not valid for current subscribers to Harlequin Presents books. All orders subject to credit approval. Credit or debit balances in a customer's account(s) may be offset by any other outstanding balance owed by or to the customer. Please allow 4 to 6 weeks for delivery. Offer available while quantities last.

**Your Privacy**—The Harlequin® Reader Service is committed to protecting your privacy. Our Privacy Policy is available online at www.ReaderService.com or upon request from the Harlequin Reader Service.

We make a portion of our mailing list available to reputable third parties that offer products we believe may interest you. If you prefer that we not exchange your name with third parties, or if you wish to clarify or modify your communication preferences, please visit us at www.ReaderService.com/consumerchoice or write to us at Harlequin Reader Service Preference Service, P.O. Box 9062, Buffalo, NY 14269. Include your complete name and address.

"HAVE *you* changed, Poppy?" This time when he spoke her name the word emerged crisp and clear, yet he tasted the echo of it on his tongue, sweet as wild raspberries but with a tang of disappointment.

How was it that after all this time she had the power to make him *feel*?

It must be some residual weakness after his ordeal in the wilderness.

"Of course I've changed." He heard her long stride across the floor as she paced. "I'm not twenty-three anymore. I'm my own woman, self-reliant, secure and capable."

"You were always self-reliant," he murmured. "You never needed anyone, did you, Poppy? Except on your own terms." He heard her hiss of breath. "You used people for what you could get. Is that still your style?"

"You're a fine one to talk! When did you ever *give* or share?"

Orsino heard her jagged breath and knew intense satisfaction that he wasn't the only one *feeling*.

"I remember giving all the time." He breathed deep. "Money, the prestige and connections you were so hungry for…"

Silence met his accusation. He waited, but she didn't break it.

So, in one thing at least she'd changed. Once she'd been ruled by passion, as impetuous in her defence as in everything else. Now she knew when to give up. What was the point arguing the unwinnable?

Orsino frowned, fighting a disappointment he couldn't explain.

"Obviously you don't want me here." Her voice sounded guarded and, if he hadn't known it impossible, defeated. "The hospital made a mistake contacting me."

He shook his head, wishing yet again that he could see her face. The strength of his need to see her stunned him.

"No mistake. But they were a little too prompt. You're not needed quite yet."

"Needed? You don't need me."

Orsino heard the shock in her voice and didn't bother hiding his smile. Maybe it was shallow of him but after all this time, after what she'd done, it felt good to have her exactly where he wanted her.

"But when I leave the hospital I will. Who else should look after me as I recuperate but my wife?"

\* \* \*

*Step into the gilded world of* **The Chatsfield!**
*Where secrets and scandal lurk behind every door…*
*Reserve your room!*
*November 2014*